"A major talent is revealed in this debut novel, a work that combines the hallucinatory quality of D. M. Thomas's *The White Hotel,* the enigma of a Talmudic fable, the charm of a Yiddish folk tale and the lyric surrealism of a Chagall painting . . . Skibell's masterful skill in maintaining the thin line between fantasy and reality and between sorrow and bitterness, his deft interjection of gallows humor and poetic passages of gossamer delicacy, allows him to spin a story that beguiles even as it breaks your heart."

—*Publishers Weekly* (starred review)

"Skibell has given us an astonishing first novel. He has turned the full light of his extraordinary talent and vision on one of history's darkest moments and taught us to see it again."

—*The Boston Globe*

"Vivid imagery . . . robust gallows humor . . . A fine debut, manifestly infused with deep familial and cultural feeling, and a signifcant contribution to the ongoing literature of the Holocaust."

—*Kirkus Reviews*

"Oh, what a magical book. I finished it moved, enchanted, saddened, and exhilarated."

—Sister Wendy

"Utterly different and surreal, this first novel takes an original approach to the Holocaust and leaves a lasting impression."

—*Library Journal* (starred review)

(continued on next page)

A BLESSING ON THE MOON

Joseph Skibell

BERKLEY BOOKS, NEW YORK

A BLESSING ON THE MOON

A Berkley Book / published by arrangement with
Algonquin Books

PRINTING HISTORY
Algonquin Books edition / January 1991
Berkley trade paperback edition / April 1999

The Penguin Putnam Inc. World Wide Web site address is
http://www.penguinputnam.com

ISBN: 0-425-16713-5

BERKLEY®
Berkley Books are published by
The Berkley Publishing Group, a member of Penguin Putnam Inc.,
375 Hudson Street, New York, New York 10014.
BERKLEY and the "B" design are trademarks
belonging to Berkley Publishing Corporation.

PRINTED IN THE UNITED STATES OF AMERICA

10 9 8 7 6 5 4 3 2 1

My work on this novel was generously supported by a James A. Michener Fellowship from the Texas Center for Writers at the University of Texas/Austin, and the Jay C. and Ruth Hall Fellowship in Fiction from the Institute for Creative Writing at the University of Wisconsin/Madison. The first chapter appeared in a slightly different form in *Story* magazine.

Heartfelt thanks to Basha v'Ari and the Freer-Skibell-Winston mishpokheh; the faculty, staff, and my colleagues and friends in Austin and in Madison; los hombres de la junta (it sounds more dangerous than it is); the exquisite Elisabeth Scharlatt and the amazing folks at Algonquin Books; the redoubtable Wendy Weil and her staff; and the novelist James Magnuson—friend, mentor, Dutch uncle, mensh.

For my great-grandparents

Sarah and Abe Balk

Goldie and Lipman Baruch Lezanski

Gitl and Michael Mintz

Ester and Chaim Skibelski

and their children

והביאנו לשלום מארבע כנפות הארץ

And now they do not see light, it is brilliant in the skies.

—Job 37:21

For there existed suspicion that at first something that looked to them like the moon had appeared in the gathering clouds, but that the clouds subsequently disappeared and that they had seen nothing.

—RAMBAM, Sanctification of the New Moon 2:6

A BLESSING ON THE MOON

Joseph Skibell (signature)

FROM THE MAYSEH BOOK

I

It all happened so quickly. They rounded us up, took us out to the forests. We stood there, shivering, like trees in uneven rows, and one by one we fell. No one was brave enough to turn and look. Guns kept cracking in the air. Something pushed into my head. It was hard, like a rock. I fell. But I was secretly giddy. I thought they had missed me. When they put me in the ground, I didn't understand. I was still strong and healthy. But it was useless to protest. No one seemed to hear the sounds I made or see my thrashings, and

anyway, I didn't want to draw attention to myself, because then they would have shot me.

I was lying in a pit with all my neighbors, true, but I was ecstatic. I felt lighter than ever before in my life. It was all I could do not to giggle.

And later, as dusk gathered, I climbed out of the grave, it was so shallow, and I ran through the forests. Nobody saw me. I ran with the dirt still in my mouth. I had to spit it out as I ran.

When I got to our village, everything was gone. A dozen workmen were lifting all the memories into carts and driving off. "Hey! Hey!" I shouted after them. "Where are you going with those?" But they wouldn't stop. In front of every house were piles of vows and promises, all in broken pieces. How I could see such things, I cannot tell you.

A villager and his family were moving into our house on Noniewicza Street. Crouching behind a low wall, I watched them, a man and his sons, sweating through their vests. They packed and unpacked their crates, their shirtsleeves rolled up high, carting furniture in and out of our courtyard. Now and then, one would leave off to smoke, only to be derided by the others for his idleness.

I was afraid if they saw me, they would come after me. Still, I couldn't stand to see what they were doing. I called to them, my voice escaping on its own. I was shouting. I shouted their names. I couldn't help it. But they said nothing, merely continued with their hauling and their crates.

So I touched them. I grabbed onto their shoulders, I pleaded with them. At that, they crossed themselves and shuddered. They muttered their oaths. They were peasants. Superstitious. But otherwise, there was no response. And I realized I was dead. I was dead. But why was I not in the World to Come?

"Perhaps this is the World to Come."

The words came from a black crow sitting in an empty tree.

"Rebbe," I said. I recognized the voice as belonging to our beloved Rabbi. "How can that be?" I said. "Strangers are moving into my house. You yourself are a crow. How is it possible this is the World to Come?"

"Be grateful," he squawked. "Rejoice in your portion."

And he flew away.

I felt worse than before. I had nowhere to go. Still, nobody could see me, what would it matter if I went home, if I entered my own house? Why not sleep in my own bed? So back to our court on Noniewicza Street I go. In through the front door. They didn't even bother to lock it. I stand in the foyer, peering into the various rooms. I clear my throat to announce myself, but there's no doubting I'm as invisible as air.

The family is sitting around the dining-room table. They are people I know, people I have traded with. Eggs sometimes, bread, linens, goods of this sort. "Look how nice everything is," the Mama says to her sons, clapping her hands in delight. "So beautiful, Mamuśku, so beautiful," a daughter says, but she is the one they

never pay attention to, and the eldest son says over her, "A toast! To our home and to our table!" The father's face beams with pride.

Upstairs are three more sons, big snoring lummoxes, asleep in Ester's and my bed. Fully clothed they are, with even their boots on.

It's like a fairy tale from the Mayseh Book!

The rooms are filling up. And where can I sleep? They've invited all their relatives to come and settle in. No one is in the nursery and so I sleep in Sabina's little bed with my feet sticking over the edges. The bed we've kept from when her own mama, our daughter Edzia, was little and slept in the nursery as well.

Outside the window, the Rebbe pecks on the shutters to be let in. I open the sill as quietly as possible. "What was that?" a groggy voice from Lepke's old room echoes down the hall. "Mamuśku, the bed is so big, I'm swimming in it," one daughter cries. "Everyone to bed, to bed!" the Mama calls out, cross. The Rebbe circles the room, walking from side to side, his wings behind his back. "Chaim," he says. "Your legs, they stick out over the edges." I sigh. He settles onto a pillow near me. He tucks his head into his breast.

I wake up and the sun is black beneath a reddened sky. My head is pounding and my eyes hurt against the light.

Downstairs, the Serafinskis are exchanging gifts over breakfast, various things they have found in their rooms during the night. The table is festive with ribbons and all the colored packages. "Papa, oh Papa, thank you so much," the plump daughter says, leaning over

the table to kiss her father. The shift she has slept in opens and her small breasts are momentarily revealed. "Don't disturb your father while he eats!" her Mama scolds. But she herself is made so gay by Ester's pearls, which gleam around her neck, that she cannot stay mad for long.

There are pigs now in the shul, and goats. They mill about, discussing methods of underground resistance. I'm amazed I can understand their language. "Can we rely on the villagers for protection?" one of the pigs says, his voice quavering with rage. "Think again, my friends," a goat warns, shaking his grey beard, although none of them seems convinced.

I recite the morning prayers outside in the town square, then sit on a bench and throw bread crumbs to the Rebbe.

"Hamotzi lechem min ha-aretz," he squawks out the blessing before pouncing on the little I have been able to find for him. He hops onto my shoulder and cackles reassurances into my ear. He turns his head, squinting through a hard yellow eye, to judge the effect his words have on me.

I nod, I listen, but only from habit. I'm too numb to really hear.

"And will you migrate, Rebbe?" I finally ask. "Do crows migrate?"

The question has been burdening my heart.

"God willing," he caws. "With God's help. If it's God's will."

And he flies up to perch on the ledge of a high roof, spitting a shrill cry from his throat.

2

The Rebbe is not his usual self, that much is clear. Before, you could always see him, dashing through our narrow streets, his black coat flapping behind him, a holy book clutched against his spindly chest. He was everywhere at once, counseling, joking, wheedling, pressing Talmudic points into our children's stubborn skulls. Now, I crane my neck to look at him hopping about the roof of the Hotel Krakowski, his bone-like feet curling and uncurling around its rusted gutter pipe. How distracted he looks, how ruffled and how weary. He doesn't understand our new condition, I fear, or its dangers. Were it not for a small collection of pebbles I've taken to flinging at them, for instance, the Rebbe might easily have been devoured by any number of neighborhood cats. "Shoo! Go away! Scat!" I cry. "Are you crazy?" I shout at them. "Do you want to *eat* the Rebbe!" And they slink off, chastened, licking their wounded paws.

The soldiers seem to like our town, with its sleepy squares and the many bridges crossing its rivers. The worst of their work is over and they can finally relax and enjoy their stay. I stroll among them with my cane, searching for the ones who shot us, but their faces are unrecognizable. Gone are the tight grimaces, the tensed piano wires that stood up in their necks when they barked out their commands. Now they are all sunniness and light, and even when they catch someone hiding in a garret or a cellar, they are able to beat

and kick the poor wretch happily and shoot at him as though it were all a trifling canard, without unpleasant yelling.

This is how it was with Lipski the butcher. The woman he had traded his house to for a hiding place reported him at once. And who can blame her? With Lipski curled into a circle below her staircase, she was in danger and her family as well. But the soldiers danced him out in that jolly way of theirs, flushing him so merrily from his hutch and into the bright streets that even Lipski had to laugh, as they beat his head into the curb.

In the late afternoon, a thin man in a homburg stands upon a hastily erected platform to give a ringing speech. He congratulates our town on its spirit of heroic cooperation.

"Never before . . ." he pounds his delicate fist against the podium.

"So often in . . ." he cries.

"Young men giving . . ." he thunders.

I try to listen, but the words are lost on me. The crowd pushes forward eagerly. Men from the region's newspapers jot down notes in little books, to print in their papers the following day. So busy is everyone listening to the speech that no one notices a large black bird swooping down, like a shadow, from the trees to peck at the speechmaker's eyes. A purplish iridescent whirl descends about the poor man's hat and he raises two bloodied fists to protect his shredded cheeks. Those near to him laugh, once, as people will, before realizing the true extent of his distress. Recovering their somberness, they move in from all sides, offering their help. The mayor,

various townspeople, more than a dozen soldiers swat at the Rebbe, but no one is able to stop him as he tears the man's finger from his hand and flies towards the forests, a golden wedding band glinting in his beak.

3

"Rebbe! Rebbe!" I run through the crowd after him, the guns shooting over my head. Away he flies, deep into the forests, far from our little town. That I am able to run so fast, a man of my age, it's difficult to believe, even with the aid of my stick. The trees, black against the darkening sky, scratch at my collar and tear at my neck. I keep tripping over roots and stones, the forest is tangled and so dense.

"Rebbe," I shout up at him. "You have stolen something that doesn't belong to you, something that must be returned! This isn't proper!"

But on he sails, high above the treetops, ignoring my every word.

I follow him into a small clearing, where he begins gliding in circles, his wings long and stiff. He lands unsteadily near a small pond and struts on his wiry legs to the water's edge. A twitch of his head and the ring is tossed in with a gentle liquid *plink!*

"Rebbe," I say, laughing. "What a terrible thief you are! If you had

wanted to conceal your crimes, you should have dropped it from the air above the middle of the pond. But now, let me see what have you stolen."

I reach into the water.

The blues and the pinks of twilight stain the surface of the pond, and through them I see, for the first time since I was shot, a reflection of my face. One side is entirely missing, except for an eye, which has turned completely white. Barely hanging in its socket, it stares at itself in an astonished wonder. My grey beard is matted thick with blood, and broken bits of bone protrude here and there through the raw patches of my flesh.

I look like a mangled dog carcass.

The Rebbe squawks.

"Why have you shown me this?"

"Chaim, Chaim, Chaim," he shrills in a piping tone. "Never in my life have I behaved like such an animal! What has happened to me? And look at you! Look what they have done to your face!"

"Rebbe," I say, "Rebbe," comforting him.

He caws softly. I suppose he is unable to cry. I nuzzle the top of his black head against my partial cheek.

Inside the ring, I see, is a small inscription. *To Johannes From His Margarite, Undying Love*. I slip it onto my finger so that I will not lose or misplace it before it can be returned.

Shadows gather in from behind the trees, inking the forests,

until everything is black. Wolves snicker somewhere not far off. Together, the Rebbe and I offer up our evening prayers. He sits upon my shoulder and we walk home beneath a bright canopy of stars.

4

That night and for many nights after, I am unable to sleep. I toss and turn in Sabina's little bed, haunted by the queerest dreams. Not visions, as one might expect. Instead, I *feel* the approach of others near me, reaching out to me from all sides. My arm is tucked beneath my head, dangling off the bedside. Playfully, they grab onto my hand, curling their fingers around my own. This tickling awakens me. I sit up, laughing, barely understanding why. "There they are again," I say. It's a little frightening as well. The covers fall to my lap and I peer curiously into the room, searching every corner, but all I see are blue abstract blotches moving about in the moon-filled dark. My eyes adjust to the dimness and the shapes disappear altogether.

The Serafinskis sleep throughout the house. Relatives and family friends fill every bed, every sofa, every chair. From all corners, their monstrous breathing rises and falls, vibrating through throats so thickened with sleep, it sounds like a mass drowning.

I replace the blankets over the Rebbe's fluttering chest and stand for a moment at the nursery door, wide awake, listening. My fingers

fumble uselessly in the pockets of my nightclothes, worrying a small bead of lint. When I was alive, often on a night like this, if I couldn't sleep, I'd make my way downstairs to the kitchen and grind up beans for coffee. Ester, beside me in our bed, would barely budge as I noiselessly extracted myself from her grip. A tall woman, she shrunk with age and grew stout. The lines in her face were deeply cut and, even in her sleep, she scowled. Ten children had hidden themselves in her body and, over the years, at regular intervals, one by one, they crawled out. Sarah first, then Itzhak and the others, Edzia, Shlomo, Izekial, Miriam, Hadassah, then Laïbl, Shmuel, and Eliahu. My first wife, Ida, could have no children, and died trying.

I navigate the passage to the kitchen easily in the dark. Despite all the furniture and crates carted through my foyer, the house is remarkably unchanged. I have no idea where they've stowed everything. I pass all their children's bedrooms. Their bodies lie twisted, like shipwrecks, in the sheets, as though a great sea had tossed them there. Down the back stairway, to the bottom floor, I press lightly against the kitchen's oaken door to muffle its notorious creaking. Foolish, I know, these precautions. Why take them? Who am I afraid of waking? It's beyond their ability to harm me now. Still, what good would rousing them from their drunken slumbers do? Let them sleep, let them sleep. It's enough, having the house to myself for a night. Soon, morning will pry its way through their windows, forcing its light into their bleary eyes, and soon enough, the

harsher light of their own bad conscience will surely stir them with its sharper prick. After all, how long can they continue to live so gaily in another man's house before one of them sobers up and convinces the others to draft a letter immediately to its rightful heirs?

In the kitchen now, grinding the coffee, it occurs to me to write this letter myself. With the Rebbe's help, perhaps I can get a note to one of my sons. Sign it with one of the Pole's names and include the lease and the thick stack of legal papers. Who would ever know? Surely the Rebbe will aid me in posting it. He's always finding bits of string here and there, useful odds and ends, and many things for tying up a parcel.

I sit against the kitchen window, contemplating my plan and gazing up into the night sky. My coffee is long cold. Apparently, I cannot drink it. One more of the disadvantages of being dead. I had spiked the cup with whiskey, hidden years ago in a cupboard, which not even the villagers with their drinker's noses had managed to sniff out. If only I were drunk, then I would dance around the parlor in my nightshirt, circling around the villagers as they lie, snoring, with their legs and arms sprawled across the sofas and the chairs. Ah, what a fright I could give them! If only they would see me. Whirling around and around, I accidentally knock over a lamp from a side table with the bottle in my hand. "Hunh? Wah?" one of them mutters. He looks about him in the dark, his face lanky with sleep. But he only shrugs and closes his eyes. He clacks a heavy tongue against the roof of his mouth and is snoring once again.

I ascend the stairs and make my way to the nursery and crawl into bed, hoping that the Rebbe might be awake, so that I may tell him of my plans for the letter to my sons. But he isn't there. The little bed is empty and a small, warm depression is all that remains. Because he complains that I move around too much in my sleep, he has been building a nest for himself behind the old rocking horse, where it is unlikely anyone will find it. I move the horse and a tin ball and a small mechanical monkey to see if he is there, but his unfinished nest is empty as well. There is a note written in a scrawl I cannot decipher. A sharp cry pierces the night outside the open window. The curtains move. With my hands on the casement, I lean far into the purple darkness, but can see nothing. I stare up at the full moon and, to my astonishment, it falls from the sky! The orange ball simply sinks and disappears behind the trees.

5

In my office, I have found a ledger book beneath a number of things in the back of an old desk drawer. Now that the Rebbe is gone and I have no one else to talk to, I have taken to crossing the courtyard and spending my nights here alone. The office is exactly as I left it. Or so it appears to me. If someone has changed it in the meantime, it's impossible to say how. As always, the maps of the river routes, along which we sent our lumber, are still in place, still in their

frames along the walls. My wooden humidor still rests upon my large oak desk, although, of course, without breath, smoking is a bitter and a useless frustration.

Here, no one intrudes and I can sit with my feet on the desk and lean back. I can stare out over the Niemen and the Bobre and watch the dawn begin above their moving waters. Or I can sleep on the daybed, undisturbed.

Even if I oversleep, the new owners, of course, do not see me. Usually, I'm up and out well before their workday commences. But once or twice, I shuffled out of my office as many of my old employees were shuffling in. For a moment, so vivid is the impression of being alive and among them in my old place, that I very nearly greet them.

"So you survived, did you?" I can almost hear them say. Mendel the office clerk takes my walking stick, and the staff manager my hat. "Welcome back, welcome back! Everything is as you left it. Grab the boss a cup of coffee, would you, Felice? Hurry up! Hurry up!" and my life resumes, exactly where it left off, as though I had not died, but only journeyed to see my daughters in Warsaw or in Lodz.

"So you survived then, did you?" the staff manager asks ironically, taking my hat and handing my stick to the clerk. He follows me to my office, inadvertently stepping on my heels. "I have daughters, too, as you know, as you well know," he says. "And grandchildren, grandchildren! How they can devour you! But you survived, and

thank God for that. Visits to one's relatives can be treacherous, treacherous."

I imagine myself joking with him, not impatiently as usual, my mind already half on work, but warmly, even sentimentally, as though the tiring familiarity of his worn jests could somehow knit my broken body and return me to my former life.

But, no. On those mornings when I have slept too long on the daybed and have arisen to find the office staff settling in for another day, I pass among them unnoticed, unfelt, possibly unremembered, not unlike all their colleagues who disappeared that day into the pit. To them, it is no different than if I had sold the business and taken half the workers with me. We are gone. Simply. No one cares where.

I try to put these thoughts in the ledger book on the nights when I can't sleep. I sit at my desk, threading through its pages, my right hand caressing each sheet slowly, each line with a methodical and even stroke. Its first few pages are dotted with numbers, we had only begun the new year, and many of the pages towards the back have children's drawings on them, left, I'm certain, by my grand-children. When my own children were small, I allowed them to draw and paint in the unused portions of these books. Round lemony suns. Blue rhomboidal houses. Winged horses grazing in fields of red wheat. It became a family tradition. It did no harm as far as I could see but, for some reason, it distressed my accountants, Shumski and Matulski.

"These are not toys, Pani Chaim!" Matulski rails.

"These are your company's ledgers!" Shumski needlessly points out.

"Official documents," Matulski stresses.

"What will people think?"

"What people?" I tell him. "You and Matulski are the only ones who see these books."

"And what will *we* think?" says Shumski, hiding behind his glasses.

"Exactly," rails Matulski.

"But if it makes the children happy," I try to console them.

"That there have been children drawing in these books, *children!*" Shumski points wildly at the floor. "That's what Matulski and I will think!"

For myself, I rather like the little drawings. I write the story of Shumski and Matulski right over the flying boat and a sleeping moon Izzie or Solek must've drawn. Absentmindedly, I find I have even added my own sketch—an inky portrait of Shumski and Matulski flailing their arms at me in disgust, throwing their hands into the Heavens.

But I have been daydreaming. It must be late. Although I carry my pocketwatch, the numbers no longer make any sense to me. The golden sticks whirl around and around, chasing each other, but I have forgotten how to understand the little races they daily perform.

Sighing, I close the ledger book. Its heavy leather casing is cool to the touch. Although my senses have survived intact, since my death I must say the sensation of touch never ceases to surprise me. Holding the closed book before me, I see several tiny convex reflections of my ruined face in the bright brass buttons that form a border around the binding. I hide the book away for the night, tucking it under the cushions of the daybed, and go out to stroll along the river.

Still the moon has not returned.

6

The bleeding has begun again. There is apparently nothing I can do. I imagine I have lost everything and am completely drained, when I feel it gurgling down my neck, leaking from the wounds in the back of my head. The spillage collects inside my shirt collar and I tighten my necktie in the hopes of stanching its flow. Because I no longer breathe, I'm able to pull the knot remarkably tight. But the blood simply reroutes itself and emerges from the star-like pattern of holes across my back and chest. It drains into my pockets and pools there, eventually cascading over like a fountain. My shoes fill with the stream issuing from my anus. My feet slide and stick in the puddles I leave, until the shoes pull off, despite the suction created by

the fluids in them. I hobble around, searching for a comfortable position and, like a tubercular uncle, I leave scores of dampened handkerchiefs, little poisoned roses, all about the house.

Instead of suffering politely and considerately this time, waiting for the wounds to drain, in the tub, for instance, or in the garage with my old car on top of the straw, I walk through the house, leaving trails in the hallways, through the rooms, on the staircases. I roll around like a dog on its back in the beds, smearing the sheets. I leave red handprints on the patterned wallpaper, at every level, so they cannot be missed. Crimson palm prints on their family photographs. They've lined them up on the mantels of the fireplaces and on the piano top. For these, I rummage with two fingers inside my opened skull, leaving bits of brain in the stain like a painter's impasto.

I open the kitchen drawers and shake my moistened sleeves over their utensils and their pots. My blood rains down in a vibrant cascade. May they eat with it in their mouths!

I mark a slanted vermilion slash across every lintel and on the doorposts of their house, and upon their gates. But, of course, they do not see it.

They never will.

A cup out of place or a toppled lamp, these they notice and shrug over, but my blood is invisible to them.

Eventually, my fury abates and I am exhausted. I struggle but can

barely keep my eyes open. My throat burns. It's on fire, like a burning desert. This is how it is every time I bleed.

I stumble up the stairs, holding on to the railings for support. My socks, slick with the drying blood, slip on every other stair and I bang my knees and shins when I fall. Drowsy, my head spinning, I drop, barely conscious, in a heap, like a bag of soiled laundry, on the threshold of the nursery. Across the room, the white sheets of Sabina's tiny bed look like a brilliant snowy mountain. My emptied wounds burn as the air whistles through them, whistling through the drying passages in my body's empty cavity. If only I could sink into the bed, into that mountain of white, and lie in its cooling sheets, like a hiker stranded beneath an avalanche, forgetting everything, even my name. But unpleasantly I am awakened.

One of the daughters is screaming.

7

"Mama! Mama! Mama!" she shrills.

"Ola, calm down!"

"Blood! Everywhere!"

"Ola, what is it?"

"Everywhere! Mama, it's everywhere!"

"There is no blood. Look! There is no blood!"

"Mama, you're covered with it! Mama, the house! All the houses in the courtyard, Mama, look!"

All the houses in the courtyard? I wasn't that ambitious. Clearly, the poor girl is raving.

"You're dreaming, Ola. Little Ola, you're dreaming."

The daughter, quivering in her mother's thick arms, twitches in convulsive spasms, as she tries to wipe my blood off her translucent shift.

"Mama, please, it's in my mouth. Mama!"

"Ola, enough of this nonsense. Andrzej, help me!"

And the Papa trundles up the stairs, annoyed to be called away from his game of Sixty-Six. He wipes his hands against his vest.

"What am I supposed to do?" he bellows. "What's wrong with her?"

"Papa, the hallways are filled with blood!"

"Put her to bed, Andrzej. Help me carry her at least!"

Together, they lift the skinny girl by her arms and her legs. She flails uselessly against them, crying out. I watch through one eye, my head on Sabina's bed, the dried blood causing my ear to stick to the pillowcase. I fall asleep again, but am wakened moments later. The Mama and Papa have laid the poor girl into bed, but of course there is blood over all the sheets and her shrieking has started again. She is nearly out of her mind. Finally, a slap and some harsh words from Papa put a stop to the whole drama, followed by the daughter

breathing too fast to catch her breath. The Mama and the Papa thump down the hallway, bumping into one another, passing accusations back and forth between them like an unwanted shoe.

". . . she's always been this way . . ." ". . . but she's sick. You shouldn't have hit her . . ." ". . . blood in the hallways. Ridiculous!" ". . . how long is she going to be sick? She can't stay in bed her entire life . . ." ". . . it's not her fault if she sees these things!" ". . . you spoiled her. So of course, it's not her fault . . ." ". . . you're the one who insisted she was too frail to work. Me, I wanted to hire her out long ago!"

Ola is curled up in a rocking chair, sucking her thumb, shivering, staring through the window, although there is really nothing to see from where she sits, besides an empty sky. I have dragged myself along the corridor to take a peek at her. I lean against her door, grab onto the knob and raise myself up. I see her through the keyhole. She is about thirteen or fourteen, with large black patches underneath her eyes. Her skin is pale with red blotches and her brown hair lies lank and stringy against her bony shoulders. The shoulders, like her knees, which are pulled up to her chest, have little knobs on them. Did I say her chest is bony? It's practically concave.

Her weeping is interrupted by a coughing fit so violent it nearly shakes her off her chair. She covers her mouth with two flat hands. Her knobby elbows rise and fall against the sides of her chest. Her throat scrapes against itself like a rusty hinge.

When she lowers her hands from her mouth, they are smeared with a bright pink blood. "Oh God," she moans. "Oh God." I look on, horrified, as she rubs the blood violently across her face and into her hair.

8

The day is clear and crisp. The chilled smells of autumn fill the air. Lonely and with nothing else to do, nothing to keep myself occupied, I have come for a stroll in the forest. The sun pours its thickened light, like honey, through the trees. It must be nearing the month of Cheshvan, but without the moon, who can tell for sure?

I'm not certain what draws me here, to the mound the soldiers made when they covered our pit. I had worried the place might be difficult to find, but the ground virtually rolls and buckles from the bluish gases erupting in balloons beneath my feet.

Leaning on my cane, I lower myself and sit upon the mound. I haven't been here since I climbed out, scrambling over the edge, looking back only once, and quickly at that. Their bodies, still writhing, lay twisted in great heaps like so many pieces of a jigsaw puzzle, unassembled, on a parlor table.

The wind blows carelessly through the trees, tearing the leaves from their branches. I dig with my fingers, softly, into the dirt.

My lumber business used to bring me to all parts of the forest, but looking about now, I can't recall if I was ever here.

It's not a long walk from our house and yet it must have been more strenuous than I had at first thought, for suddenly, I find I have no strength at all and can barely remain sitting up. I lean over, lowering my ear to the ground, resting my head against it.

Faintly at first, but then more and more distinctly, I'm able to make out the sounds of Yiddish being spoken. How is this possible? I crawl about the mound, keeping my ear flat against it. Directly below me, mothers are clacking out tart instructions to their daughters. I nearly weep to hear it! To my left, there must be a cheder, for a class is clearly going on. The teacher remonstrates with his students, spitting out the alef-bais for the hundredth time. Below me, to my right, two men argue passionately. About what, at first it's difficult to hear. But so persistent are they, each one repeating his entrenched position over and over again, that soon I understand their disagreement concerns the price of trolley fares in Warsaw. I laugh, holding my sides with joy. I can't believe it. In a far corner, a deep voice drones a portion of the Mishnah in a lilting cantillation. How long has it been since I've heard the mother tongue!

"Landsmen! Landsmen!" I cry out to them.

"Who's that?" "Who is that up there?" "Reb Chaim, is that you?" The voices come at once.

"It's me! It's Chaim Skibelski!" I shout. "Is that you, Reb Motche? Who is that?"

"Reb Chaim, what are you doing out there?" Reb Motche asks me, amazed.

"I thought I'd visit you!" I say, laughing.

"You're alive then? Yes? You survived?"

"Not really, no."

"And the Rebbe?" another voice asks.

"One at a time, one at a time!" someone shouts thickly.

"He's well. He's alive, God be praised! He's well."

"Chaim?" Yet another voice.

"Yes, who is it?"

"This is Reb Elchonon."

"Elchonon! Praise God! How are you?"

"Reb Mendele and I have a question for you concerning trolley fares."

"And your family, Reb Chaim," his daughter Tsila Rochel interrupts him bluntly. "Where are they? We don't see them here."

"In Warsaw. Ester and my daughters are in Warsaw and in Lodz, and also my two sons. The others, of course, are in America, thank God."

Not knowing what to do, I had bundled Ester up and, together, we boarded the train for Warsaw. A city is safer, we thought, bigger, a Jew less conspicuous there. We'll be with our daughters, and besides, people are more civilized in a city, even the Poles. Unfortunately, we arrived only to discover that she had gone to Suwalk, our Mirki, in search of us! Our trains must have

crossed paths, each on separate tracks. Immediately, I reboarded the train to bring her back, only to arrive in Suwalk on the night that the police went round, knocking on the doors where the soldiers slept, telling them where to go in the morning with their guns.

"Reb Chaim," someone calls up. "Why are we not in the World to Come?"

"The Rebbe will explain it when he returns," I say. "The important thing is to be of good cheer."

"Where *is* the Rebbe, Reb Chaim?"

I shout into the ground, "The Rebbe will explain everything, everything, when he returns."

How can I tell them that the Rebbe became a crow and flew away?

AT HOME, ANDRZEJ and his cousins are playing cards. A bottle of potato vodka stands in the middle of their green-felt card table. There are small tumblers for everyone.

"If the yids want the moon," Big Andrzej says, removing one of my best cigars from between his teeth, "then what's it to us?" His lips are full and wet and his face, I notice for the first time, is not altogether unpleasant. "Let them keep it," he says. "They're the only ones who ever used it. It's not as if they took the sun."

"Now that *would* be a crime," his wife says, moving through the room with an armful of dirty plates.

"But Andrzej," one of the innumerable cousins looks up from his cards with a disagreeable face. "It simply isn't fair," he says. "They have no right to it. What will happen to the tides? And to women's cycles?"

The cousins laugh. "And what do you know about women's cycles, Miroslaw?"

"Not enough to pump up the tires!"

"But Miroslaw, look at all they gave us!" Andrzej gestures about the room with two sturdy arms. "And you're going to begrudge them the moon?"

"How do we even know they're the ones that took it?" cousin Stanislaw puts in.

Andrzej nods and grunts, encouraging the talk. It's evident he's enjoying the conversation.

Jaroslaw replies, "The yids disappear and the moon disappears and you're telling me they didn't take it?"

"Where *are* the yids anyway?" cousin Zygmunt insists.

"What do you care?"

"Maybe whoever took the yids took the moon?"

"Possible, it's possible," Bronislaw murmurs.

"So? So what? Who cares?" Andrzej barks, dealing out a new hand.

"But Andrzej, you think they'll stop with the moon?" cousin Zygmunt says. "Soon they'll want the stars and then the entire planetary system!"

"The soldiers have been asking around."

"So what do they know?"

"They may think *we* took it."

"Don't tell them anything."

"The whole thing gives me the creeps," says Zygmunt and he pretends to shiver.

"But we don't use it, Zygmunt!" Andrzej nearly shouts. "It's a useless little nothing of a planet. There's no purpose in making a government case!"

9

She no longer bathes, this Ola, and barely eats. Her room is locked from the inside and no one knows how she clears her bowels.

"I'm leaving a pot near the door! Do you hear, Ola?" the Mama calls through the wall but, of course, a reply is denied her. There is no answer of any kind. I'm in the hallway, tapping my palms against the head of my walking stick, curious how the confrontation will turn out. With so much time on my hands, it's only too easy to involve myself with gossip and trivia and matters of fleeting consequence such as the Serafinski family drama. During my life I gave no time to such things, and now to think that I'm wasting my death on them! But how else am I to fill my days?

The Mama has given up all hope. She leaves the pot in the hall, and her heavy body trudges down the staircase. A moment later, the door to Ola's room opens soundlessly and a skinny grey arm slinks through the crack, like a blind eel, to retrieve the copper pot. The smells that escape from the room are overwhelming and I clutch a blood-smeared kerchief to my nose.

"Is that you, Ola? Are you coming down?" "Let her stay up there until she rots!" "Shhh, Andrzej, shhh, she'll hear!" "But Mamuśku, her room stinks." "Both of you, enough! She'll hear, she'll hear!" "Let her. What do I care if she hears?"

Their competing voices rush, as if racing, to the top of the stairs, but the click of the lock on Ola's door silences the house, leaving only their furtive whisperings to continue on below.

Stealthily, I creep over to Ola's door, protecting my nostrils with the cloth, and peer again through the little keyhole. I should be ashamed of myself, and yet my curiosity will not let me rest. What I see unnerves me. The girl is shivering, wrapped in a dirty bedsheet. She sways from side to side in the rocking chair. So thin is she that the light from the windows nearly shines through her greyish skin. Her body contracts into itself, her knees rise up and her elbows lock into her chest. She wheezes like an ancient bellows, coughing up a bloody plug of phlegm. There is slime and feces all about the floor and even on the bed.

"Enough, Ola! Open the door at once!"

So mesmerized had I become staring at this hellish sight that I failed to notice the father, Big Andrzej, standing over me, pounding with his clenched white fists against the door.

"Ola, do you hear!"

"Murderer!" she shouts.

"Ola!"

"Murdering pig!"

"You're making yourself sick over nothing!"

"I hate you, hate you! Do you hear me? Go away!"

Andrzej leans his heavy bulk against the doorframe, a small craft turned back by the gales of his daughter's stormy emotions. He opens a hand to pull at his big black mustache. I pity him, I can't help myself, daughters can be difficult and these villagers are simple people, peasants unused to the spirits of high-strung girls. Cutting wood, milking cows, slaughtering pigs, these are things they think a normal child should be doing.

"You're too sensitive, Ola!" her Papa shouts. "Couldn't stand to see a goose lose its head. Your mother spoils you, it's true! Filling your brains with such useless rot. Until not even a good thrashing will help. With the others, yes, but not with Ola! No, with you, it had the opposite effect. Each thrashing only made you more sullen and resentful." He tromps down the stairs in a blue cloud, annoying thoughts buzzing about his head like flies. "But it's a brutal world, God knows!" If only he could be indifferent, he probably tells him-

self, and soon enough he will attempt, through drink or lovemaking or a good solid fight, to make himself so.

"Life is too short, Ola, too short and too hard to care about such things," he thunders at the bottom of the stairs, throwing his arms this way and that in a flamboyant despair. There is something annoyingly theatrical about the family Serafinski, it's starting to grate upon my nerves. "Blubbering over some silly people who'd do the same to us—yes, Ola, to us—to your mother and to your father and to you—given half the chance!"

No sound emerges from Ola's room to answer his petty grumblings, and although I tell myself it is none of my business, the girl concerns me, and so I lay out my handkerchief before her door and am on my knees once again, peering through her keyhole. She's not well. She needs looking after, this Ola, not taunts and threats and the blistering reproaches they pour upon her head. My brow presses against the cold metal of the doorknob plate and for a moment I have the dizzying impression of staring into the center of a whirling cyclone spinning in a green-grey sea. A pink curtain drops across the image and it disappears. The cyclone reappears almost instantly and I understand that I have been looking not at the sea but directly into a human eye. She's on the other side of the door, peering out.

The door opens before I can rise from my knees and hobble away, even though I have my stick to hoist me. I was a large man, with a heavy girth, and nearly sixty besides.

"So it *is* you," she says, standing over me.

I confess I'm unprepared for the sound of her voice. It enters my ear oddly, as though I were a traveler or an explorer who left his home long ago and meets by chance a countryman who now addresses him in their native tongue. This is the first time since my death that a living person has spoken directly to me. It's impossible that she can see me, and yet the sorrow in her grey-green eyes, as she gazes over my face, bending down now on one knee and pressing my hands into hers, is enough to break my heart. Embarrassed, I straighten my coat.

"I am sorry to have troubled you," I say, attempting to stand, not knowing where to look. "You're ill. Allow me to apologize and to help you into bed."

But she strokes my raw cheek with the back of her stained hand.

"Look at you," she says. "So this is what we've done."

"It's nothing," I say. "You're ill. Let me help you to your bed."

But before I know it, she has collapsed and is weeping in my arms. I rock her, like a baby. She's burning with fever. I sit, my legs folded, on the threshold to her room, murmuring and stroking her softly.

"Sha, sha, kind," I say. Hush, hush, little one.

If only I could remember a lullaby, a nice little tune, then I would sing it to her.

10

I carry her to her bed. "I must strip the sheets," I tell her, searching for a clean spot to lay her down. Unfortunately, there is none, and so I carefully place her into the rocking chair. I hang my coat on a peg behind the door and roll up my shirtsleeves to get to work. She is shivering uncontrollably. The winter sun presses its chilling light against the room's windows, offering little heat. Despite this, Ola's brow is flushed with sweat. I can almost hear the bones of her knees clanking together. With the clattering of her teeth and the whistling sighs her quivering chest forces from her lungs, she sounds like a train disappearing down a ghostly track and I doubt that she will live much longer.

"You mustn't trouble yourself, Pan Skibelski." She holds up a nervous arm in protest. It shakes wildly in the space between us. "We are intruders here. We have no rights."

"Nonsense," I say, taking freshly laundered sheets from the linen cupboard in the hall. "I was spying on you. It's I who had no right and you who must forgive me."

She cries again and I pretend not to notice. Instead, I busy myself with the bedclothes, tucking in the corners of the sheets, fluffing the blanket in the air before me, like a magician snapping his magic cape. It settles down onto the bed and I do the same with the goose-down comforter, a gift for my Hadassah's dowry, which in-

explicably disappeared at the time of her wedding. "Ah, so this is where you've been hiding," I say to it, finding it lurking furtively in the bottom of an oaken wardrobe filled with blankets, pillows, and towels.

I leave the soiled sheets in the laundry basket at the end of the hall. In the bathroom, I fill the sink with steaming hot water, watching my reflection disappear behind the wall of mist that soon coats the mirror's glass. I drop six white hand towels into the water and then remove them and wring them out, burning my hands. I drape each one over a bare forearm, three on each side. The sensation is not unpleasant. The towels lightly singe the hair on my arms. I carry along a pewter basin into which I will drop each towel after it is spent. In my vest and shirtsleeves, I remind myself of a waiter in a posh restaurant on Warsaw's Marszal-kowska Street.

Quietly, I open the door to her room. She is curled up in the rocking chair, still, her eyes red, her cheeks drawn, sucking on a thumb encrusted with her own filth.

"You mustn't," I say, removing her hand from her mouth. I rub it with the hot cloth, wiping the dirt away. "Feels good, doesn't it?" Her body loses some of its tension, and she allows me to move the cloth across her arms. I kneel before her. She places one foot on my shoulder, and I clean the grime from her shins.

Her crying has stopped and her breathing is longer, deeper, more

regular. My hot towel scurries across her bony shoulders and her spindly neck and then into the intricate crevices of her faintly smiling mouth.

Crossing her arms, she reaches for the hem of her soiled shift, and with one move, raises her hipbone from the seat of the chair, pulling the garment off over her head. I lift a new handcloth from my forearm and quickly smooth it over her flat belly and her equally flat chest.

Her shivering returns and so I drape my jacket about her thin shoulders, while I look through my daughter's things for a clean chemise. Half asleep in the middle of the room, Ola stands with her arms in the air. I draw the clean garment over her. She yawns happily as I position her in her bed, then rolls over and is immediately asleep, her body curled into a question mark.

It is night outside. Incredible that so much time has passed. I gather my things from the room, my coat with its bullet holes, the half dozen white towels, all cold now with a heavy dampness, and I douse the light and shut the door, returning the water bowl to its place beneath the bathroom sink.

In the nursery, I hang my coat on the back of a miniature chair, lay the towels out to dry across the proscenium arch of a toy theatre. I untie my tie, unlock my cuff links, unbutton and remove my shirt. My big belly is white and round in the starlight. A forest of grey hairs grows across the soft mounds of my chest. I undo my belt and my pants sink of their own weight to my ankles. My arms and legs are long and thin, like sticks. I sit on Sabina's little bed, remove

my underpants and consider my sex. It shrivels and recoils flaccidly into its wiry nest, embarrassed by its own presence in the open air.

I quickly find my nightshirt and my nightcap, cover my nakedness, bury myself beneath the blankets and pray that soon, God willing, I will sleep forever in the ground.

Sometime during the night, I am awakened by the pressure of Ola's body next to mine. She burrows against my belly in the tiny bed. Drowsily, I welcome her under the covers, uncertain exactly who she is. The bed is so small, she must struggle for some time to find a comfortable position. Neither of us is more than a little awake. Her skin is clammy with fever. I sense that if she could, she would hide here, disappearing into me, as though my heavy bulk were a hollow mountain and her restless scramblings beneath the covers an attempt to find the opening of a cave. Finally, she raises her bottom against my abdomen, but because that is not comfortable, she gradually wiggles southward until we are pressed together, with only my stiff erection between us.

I I

The Mama and Papa are astonished at the recovery she is making. Although she is still quite ill, gone are the flaring tantrums, the hallucinations, and the wretched self-abasements. Radiant now with a low fever, Ola lies in the plump white bed, attended to by a coterie

of my granddaughters' rag dolls. Twice daily, her mother scuttles a fat crab-like hand, red and raw, over Ola's brow, then off to church she scurries to thank the virgin mother and her rabbinical son for her daughter's miraculous recovery.

Upon her return, she ascends backwards up the staircase, carrying a large tray heavy with crisp hot toast, apple-orange marmalade, and milk-boiled sausages piled high. Ola is all giggles when her mother enters, and I stand unobtrusively in a corner, like a burglar or an objectionable suitor, waiting until I can safely step from behind my curtain. Not that there is any likelihood of my being seen or caught but, still, it's best that Ola's conspiratorial winks and smirks pass unregarded behind her mother's rounded back. If only out of kindness for the poor woman. Why add fear for Ola's sanity to her already heavy bag of motherly concern? She leaves the room, content and relieved, and I sit, straight backed, in a bedside chair, while Ola picks, in frustration, at her food.

For her father, Ola has nothing but contempt. He has only to stick his doughy face into the room, mustaches flying, and all the gaiety of a moment before disappears. Ola's glare is black and her arms are crossed and these are the only answers she gives to his habitual "How's my princess faring today?" The unfortunate fellow stands in an eternity of silence, half in the room, half out, waiting for her reply. Then his face darkens as well, closing up as tightly as his daughter's. The family resemblance is never more apparent than in these minutes of stone-faced glowering. He purses his moist lips,

runs his tongue along the underside of his large bristling mustache, and mutters, "All right, then," unable to look at her. "We'll see you." And he departs for another day.

"Ola, he's your father," I tell her.

Her hair is braided and she looks at me through glasses so thick that her eyes resemble two large beetles trapped beneath the lenses. "He's a murderer," she says bitterly.

"But he isn't," I say. "He hasn't killed anyone."

"The war's not over yet."

"Ola. Be reasonable."

"He's profiting from someone else's death, isn't he? Aren't we all? It's just as bad."

"Until my sons or even my daughters can reclaim it, what point is there in letting the house stand empty? The soldiers would only put their horses in it."

"But no one asked you."

"How could they, child? I was dead."

"You only say this because you think I'm going to die. The truth is, you hate having us here."

She is right, of course, on both counts. She reads my thoughts apparently as quickly as they cross what's left of my face. When I don't answer her, she attempts to consume the meal her mother carried up. I look away as she devours, without hunger, the sausages. The squalid grease pools down her chin. My eyes trace the fading brown shadows that line the wallpaper. It's bad enough

she's so young and a Gentile, but does she have to compound my guilt by gobbling down treyf? I should speak to her of this, but what can she do? Inform her mother that she will eat only ritually clean foods? Where would they find anyone to reconsecrate the kitchen and the pots? No, to mention it at all is to call into question the entire friendship, which I'm certain is illegitimate from any point of view.

She lifts the cup from the tray, rinses her mouth with the last of its contents, swallows the mixture, and wipes her lips, not on her arms this time, but on a napkin, as I have shown her, in an attempt to please me. I raise my eyes from the wooden floor. A delicate black mask frames her eyes, a shadow beneath her skin, giving her the expression of a quizzical bandit. I know she does not eat so greedily because she is recovering from whatever is inside her, killing her. No, her appetite has returned because she is in love. With me. I have become the center for her of a universe that is daily shrinking. Preposterous, I tell myself. I do not know the exact laws regarding the living's relationship with the dead, but I am certain, from any point of examination, that our liaison is unclean.

12

She has found a small collapsible telescope and a compass beneath her bed, in a toy chest one of my children must have forgotten about long ago. Her pleasure in this simple discovery is endearing to watch. She begs me to please take her to the roof to search for the moon, as soon as the night is clear, as soon as her health will permit it. Squirming around on her bed, she spies through the window on her neighbors, muttering imbecilic phrases of her own invention, which I take to be her impression of two pirates in conspiracy.

She sleeps with the compass tight in one hand and her arm curled around the spyglass, lying half in shadow outside the lamp's trembling circle of light. I sit near her bedside, attempting to catch up with my account in the ledger book, retrieved from my offices across the courtyard, but my words are as dry and my sentences as circular as wood shavings. The Rebbe has been gone now for so long that I have given up any thought of entering the World to Come. Perhaps during all the days and years of my life, when our holy men spoke of it, I had heard incorrectly or misinterpreted some vital phrase. True, I could have studied more or even asked for clarification. But my mind was too much on business and I have only myself to blame. If only I had stayed closer to the Rebbe after my death, instead of wandering around so much, perhaps I would not have missed his sudden departure. Together, we would have as-

cended, migrating through the Heavens, a joyful song in our mouths, and I would have forgotten all about this world and its travail.

Ola yawns and stretches in her sleep, mumbling nasally the phrase "empty shoes." She repositions herself in her pillows and the telescope falls to the floor with a soft, almost apologetic *clink,* the sound of yet another thing breaking. Bending over, I retrieve the cylindrical tube from the floor, raising it to my eye, and peer through it out the window. The lens has sustained a crack, not severe enough to dislodge it from its casing. I scan my town and see it, as it were, divided in two, the vein in the lens rendering everything slightly askew.

For a long time, there is nothing moving, nothing to see, but then, along the river, my eye trails a young boy running in the thickets near its banks. The sky is purple in the dawn. He flies through the grasses, as though chased, perhaps caught out too late. He hadn't expected the sun to rise so soon. Can it be that one of us is living still, hiding out somewhere along the river? The boy is carrying something, food perhaps, and when his hat blows off his head, he does not hesitate or look behind. Neither does he stop to retrieve it. Instead, he pumps his arms harder, jumps into the air, and disappears through the crack in the lens. He is gone. I search the banks but cannot find him. A silver glow seems to emanate from where he must have jumped into the reeds.

The sky changes its mind, dropping buckets of red over the blue, until finally the dawn reveals itself as a soft yellow light. Ola stirs, opens her eyes. She pushes her arms like rolling pins across her face.

"Pani Chaim," she says, putting on her glasses. "Tell me . . ."

"Yes, my Ola?"

"What happens when we die?"

"We mustn't speak of such things," I tell her. She looks worse than ever this morning, worn out, as though the effort it cost to sleep the night has exhausted her completely.

"Who will come for me?" she says, sitting up on her elbows. "Jesus or the Virgin Mother?"

It takes a moment for me to understand these words and when I do, I don't know what to tell her. She's a child, after all.

"It's not exactly like that," I say.

"But you'll be here to guide me?"

"Ola, please."

"Tell me the truth."

"What is the truth? Who knows the truth? Do I know the truth?"

"Does it hurt?"

"Such nonsense!"

"Pani Chaim?"

"No," I say, sighing brusquely. "It doesn't hurt."

How can I tell her the truth, that we wander the earth like an au-

dience at intermission waiting for the concert to resume, unaware that the musicians have long since departed for home?

"It's like listening to beautiful music," I say, trying to sound wistful.

"That's the angel song," she says knowledgeably.

Ah, but these people have such simple faith!

"Is that what it was?" I say.

"That's what the Father says."

"Yes, but you can hear it all the time," I say. "You don't have to die for that."

It's a deafening silence, I think to myself.

"If you're good," she says.

"If that's what the Father told you, then, of course, it must be so."

They fill their heads with such rot, these priests! How we feared them as children, in their black ghouls' cloaks. They'd rap our heads with knuckles as hard as rocks if they caught us so much as looking crossways at their church. We used to run by, as children, on our way to cheder, our hearts pounding against our ribs, out of fear for these black demons, certain they were neither man nor woman with their pointy beards and their wide billowing skirts.

"I've been good," she says. "Haven't I?"

"Of course you have."

"I cried when they killed you."

"I'm sure you did."

"I didn't want them to."

"Of course you didn't."

"The guns were so loud."

"Were they?" I say. "I didn't notice."

"Terribly so."

"I don't remember." And in truth I don't. "In any case," I say, "it didn't hurt."

To change the subject, I tell her a story of two pious Jews, two Hasids, who find a boat that takes them to the moon. The boat leaves the river and sails into the sky, where the night is thick with the moon's luminous tide. On the way up, the two men argue about who is to blame for what is happening to them. They blame each other, naturally. But when they arrive, they discover pots of silver waiting for them there. These they load onto their boat, which they have tethered to a long rope girdling the moon. But the silver is too heavy for the boat, and they have piled so much of it into their frail craft that the boat sinks, pulling the moon out of the sky and leaving the earth in darkness.

1 3

Because the night is finally clear, we ascend the interior staircase to the roof. Ola is so weakened that the large coat I force upon her is almost too heavy for her to wear. She kicks off the bulky leather shoes I brought for her at the first step, unable to lift them, and continues in her stocking feet. I brace her, one hand on her arm, the

other steadying her back, and slowly, a step at a time, we take the stairs. Although she must periodically stop, she refuses to sit. Instead, she presses her meager weight into me and lays her head against my chest, until she is able to summon the strength to resume.

I feel as if I am cradling a dear coatrack in my arms, so light is she and her bones so stiff, were it not for her shaking and her trembling and the fevered heat she's giving off. This I can feel in my own cheek where it meets the top of her head. My children used to hide in this staircase. We'd search for them for hours. A silly game, and soon enough we learned where we could almost always find them. Ester worried they might fall, God forbid, playing on the roof, but the roof held no interest. It was the staircase that fascinated. They called it "the tunnel," so dark it was and tantalizing with its biting cedar smells. Ester, too, liked the tunnel, but only when she was in labor and needed to walk. So many times we climbed these narrow stairs, much like Ola and myself now, me bracing Ester, gripping her arm, pressing my hand into her back. Of course, she wasn't light and stick-like like Ola, but heavy and round, like a herring barrel. I could practically have rolled her up the staircase! The walk in the night air on the roof helped to calm her, as we waited for her midwives to arrive. And on the roof is where they would find us, Ester in a heavy heap of skirts, her dark triangular eyes staring over the railings and across the town into the sky, as though

searching the Heavens for the soul of her incubating child, waiting for it to arrive in its whiteness and its purity. It took all three midwives to lift her to her feet. This they did by surrounding her, these three little sisters, a small army whose job it is to bring more life into the world. With their arrival, I am suddenly cut adrift and rendered superfluous. Rooted to the spot, I stand watching their red and yellow and green babushkas disappearing through the rooftop doorway, my Ester borne among them, as though weightless, forgetting me entirely. I might light a cigar and smoke a little before returning to my office to pretend to work until the baby is born. On the staircase now, I have a vision of myself striding across the roof of my house, a cigar clenched happily in my teeth. I am young and whole and my family is growing beneath my feet.

"Why are you crying, Pani Chaim?" Ola asks.

I'm surprised to see her face looking intently into mine, her eyes trapped and enlarged behind her thick spectacles. Moving back and forth, searching my eyes, they look not a little like butterflies attempting to awaken.

"There are tears rolling into your beard," she says, brushing them away with the back of her hand.

"We should hurry," I say, "before the night is over."

"Pani Chaim," she says.

"Yes, Ola?"

"Nothing," she changes her mind. "I'm a silly girl. It's a stupid

question." She looks so frail, this coatrack with her braids and her enormous glasses thick as whiskey tumblers, standing against the inside of the roof's doorway, hidden in its shadow, trembling, coughing. I wipe the bloody phlegm she spits up with an old handkerchief, as red as a carnation.

"There was a boy, in my school, that I liked, but . . ." She doesn't know how to finish her sentence. "I never knew what to say to get him to like me. I'm not beautiful, like your daughters."

"My daughters?" I say.

"I've seen their pictures. My father and mother hid them away, but I know where. In the garage. How beautiful they were."

I find I can barely remember their faces.

"It's just as well," she says, blushing. "Never mind. Forget it, forget it. Open the door. Please. Let's go up, let's look at the stars and see if your Hasids have returned the moon yet to the sky."

I find that my voice has fled. It's no easier knowing what to do when you're dead. What can I say to her? Nothing, nothing. She is dying and so, instead, I simply watch her, spinning around where the moonlight should be, her arms reaching out to catch the stars. The night sky is a thick lavender and the stars are cold and blue. Her breaths make small clouds as they leave her mouth. So this is what laughter *looks* like, I think to myself. She is laughing. She is laughing and I don't know why.

She opens the telescope, holds it up to her eye, and peers into the sky.

"Hey," she says. "It's cracked!"

14

Things do not go so well after that. Ola's fever returns and increases dangerously, her already disastrous weight falling even further. Late into the night, she burns like a log on the white bedsheets, giving off the faintest glow, staining the sheets with a red shadow. I can't help noticing this curiosity as I pace the three sides of her bed, my arms folded tightly against my back.

Outside, there is the clatter of a wild rain.

"Pani Chaim," she says, waking, making a hoarse effort to talk.

"Ola, no speaking, sha, save your strength." The words sound ridiculous as soon as I pronounce them. For what is she to save her strength?

"I'm burning up," she says.

I place a hand on her forehead. It's like touching a hot motor.

"I'm on fire," she says, collapsing into a convulsive fit of coughing.

"Tomorrow, the doctors," I say. "Surely they will bring you a little morphine, Ola. Tomorrow."

"But I'm on fire now, Pani Chaim. Please," she says, reaching for my fingers. "Cool towels. Please. I need something to cool me down." She snatches back her hand to hug herself as she rolls over in bed, suffocating under a heavy blanket of wheezing.

Like a sleepwalker, I find myself moving through these hallways towards the kitchen and filling up a basin with cold water and small blue sheets of ice, which I chip from the block in the icebox. I drop

six white hand towels into the basin, quickly, in order not to freeze my fingertips. Upstairs, at her bedside, I wring them out, one at a time, freezing my hands anyway. She is as pale and as still as a corpse, her little broomstick legs locked tightly around a pillow. I smile, if only to reassure myself, uncertain what this ruined body needs from me. Slowly, I lay a towel against her burning forehead. She closes her eyes and breathes in deeply, her body relaxing like a tired hound. I swab another towel along her neck and then move it beneath her shift and across the bony coat hanger of her shoulders. She coughs, but not deeply this time, and a small tear escapes from beneath her sealed eyelid.

"That feels good," she says. "So cool and good." She rolls onto her stomach, her arms braided against her chest and her abdomen. Taking a new towel from the icy basin, I swathe it across her back, along the knobby river stones of her spine. Instantly, she pulls a sharp breath in between her teeth. I guide two towels along her back, down her legs, until they are swaddling her feet.

"Again," she says, and I repeat the motion with fresh towels, returning their predecessors to the basin. She releases her arms from beneath her chest, and I rub them down with my icy cloths.

She returns to her back and, raising her shift, offers up the flat expanse of her belly. She is naked beneath the shift and I hesitate before placing the wet towel above her little sex, but feel ridiculous in doing so. I'm a dead man, after all, and old enough to be her grandfather. She's dying. And besides, my body no longer presses its lech-

erous claims on me. However, when I take the last of my cooling white towels and position it there with a matter-of-fact, if tender, frankness, her eyes again close and her neck elongates, twisting and growing flush. Her grey skin marbles and stands up in glistening goose bumps. Her chin juts towards the ceiling. Her arms tense, locking at the elbows, and she lifts her body almost imperceptibly, turning it towards me. Her long flat feet rise to find my shoulders, digging into the wings of my vest. She exhales audibly, her mouth slack, her brow knotted in serene incomprehension. Damp strands of matted hair cling limply to her head. Her mouth opens in a gaping frown and I see that her teeth are as rotten and as crooked as a rabble of thieves. I release the towel, allowing it to lay, where it has fallen, on her belly.

"Perhaps, Ola, it would be best if . . . ," but her fingers find my fugitive hand, returning it to the cloth as a jailer might a prisoner to his cell. And not unlike a prisoner, my hand obeys with a docile resignation, and even slight relief.

Soon the bed is creaking with a furious monotony. Her feet have pushed beyond the nests they made in the shoulders of my vest and her heels are digging forward now against my back. Her hands flap about her two negligible breasts like birds of prey, then fly away with bits of her innocence in their beaks. If the Rebbe returned at this moment, what a dressing down he would give me! The increasing rattle of her tubercular moaning will, I fear, return her family to the door, pounding to get in. Ola cries out and I nearly jump with

fright when her burning hands blindly find my face. Taking my head in her arms, she uses it like a pole to pull her now naked body from the bed. What she has done with her shift, I can't say. She falls into my lap with such a loose clatter of bones, that I'm afraid she may have broken one of them. She swallows to catch her breath and I can feel the pounding of her ribs against my motionless heart, against the quiet cavity of my chest. She uses the length of her arm, from her wrist to her elbow, to wipe the streams running from her nose, then slices it in the other direction, like a violin bow, to clear the tears from her eyes.

Only then do we look into each other's faces.

15

Near dawn, Ola finally sleeps. Unable to calm myself, I cross the courtyard to the garage, berating myself all the while for allowing things to go this far. Never while I lived did I place myself in such a compromising circumstance! Not that the opportunities didn't present themselves. On the contrary, how many times did Siedenberg's wife send for me in her husband's name on one slim pretext after another? Usually some far-fetched real estate scheme. I would arrive and immediately be shown into the study by the maid who would return not with Siedenberg but with Rivke, his wife, buxom in a blue or green or purple velvet dress. Fabricating apologies on

her husband's behalf—he has dashed out to this minyan, had been detained at that town council meeting—she would offer me strong Arabian coffee, brandy and mandel bread, and her company as well, until her husband might return. I would extricate myself as delicately as possible, eager not to hurt her feelings, and return to my office where I would kick myself the rest of the day for being such a coward.

The garage is dark and gloomy and I find the pictures of my daughters, as Ola said I would, hidden away in a locker filled with old rags and oily motor parts. Their faces, peering out from behind the glass, are familiar to me and yet utterly unrecognizable. Would I even notice them, I wonder, if I passed them on the street?

But Ola is correct. They are beautiful. My Hadassah, my Edzia, my Sarah, and my Miriam. Surely I would notice them, if only for their beauty, so young are they, and with such clear and open faces.

I remove the photos from inside the frames, my hands trembling, as though I were committing a theft. Once or twice, the glass falls, my hands are shaking so. The sound of its breaking is muffled, mercifully, by a dirty woven rug. Here, too, in the locker, I find pictures of my sons. All but two have sailed away for America. How long has it been since I rode with Elke, my youngest, to the harbor (after he had trifled indiscreetly with a neighbor's Gentile maid)?

There is also a family portrait. Nine of our ten children surrounding Ester and myself. We were young, we two, children ourselves or nearly, me in a long Sabbath coat, Ester in her black matron's dress. The little smirk concealing itself behind my beard now makes me wince. Was I so proud, so confident, that I thought I couldn't be touched?

Most of the pictures slide easily into my pockets. Some are postcards our children had specially made, with their pictures on them, sent from this holiday or that. I stuff my vest and coat with them. The family portrait is large, however, too large for me to carry, unless I crease it, which, of course, I cannot bring myself to do. Instead, I keep it in its frame and will hide it beneath Sabina's bed, when I get the chance.

"Look, I told you I heard something and there's glass."

I have woken Łukasz, my old porter, and his niece. They sleep in a cramped room off the garage. It's the niece who enters the garage now, wrapped in a quilted horse blanket, sleep in her worried eyes. The sight of her confuses me. She was no more than a small child the last time I saw her, playing in the timber yard, a day or two before my execution. Now, I'm astonished to see a young woman with a heavy bosom elevated by two crossed arms, which she uses to pin the blanket in its place.

Łukasz follows, drunk as usual, in a pair of winter flannels. Stopping behind her, he presses his crotch into her backside.

"Uncle, stop it!" she says, annoyed, parrying him easily. "There's something out here."

"How dare you speak to your uncle in such a way!" Łukasz rears up, bellowing like an insulted nobleman.

"Or I'll have Misha cut it off and feed it to his sergeant."

"You think that just because you're sleeping with a Russian soldier or two, you can speak to me this way! I'm your uncle, after all. I'm an old man. Have pity on me," he says, very nearly cowering in a corner.

She was a hopeless little girl when she came to us. Her dying mother was Łukasz' half-sister, or maybe his sister-in-law, I no longer remember which. Only with reluctance could we persuade him to take her in, so afraid was he that caring for a child might make him less attractive to me as an employee. Never mind he was a notorious thief as well as a drunkard and a man of petty, habitual violence. Never mind the times I had to bail him out of jail. To his fevered vodka-rotted brain, this bright little girl counted as a mark against him that might one day cost him his job.

"Look here," she says.

She's found the broken glass and the empty frames and has knelt to clean them up, carefully putting the pieces in her open hand.

"You see. What did I tell you!" says Łukasz.

"You don't believe that, Uncle."

"Can a cat open a locker?" he says. "Can a mouse?"

"Europe would be crawling with them. Poland. They'd be every-where."

"I hear him, I tell you. Every night, I swear to you, I hear him."

"When you're drunk, Uncle."

"Of course, when I'm drunk! When am I not drunk? What has that to do with it?"

It's true, it's true, I have to laugh. I took my life in my hands each time I sat beside him in our lumber truck.

"I've been drunk since I was seven years old, God seeing fit to call me as an altar boy. But in all those years, I never heard a ghost, did I?"

"Until now."

"That's it, that's it," he says, blinking rapidly.

"It's rotting your brain."

"Rubbish!"

"You can't handle it anymore. You said so yourself. And you're getting older."

"The place is haunted," he screams.

She has straightened up the mess I've left, sweeping up the smaller shards, returning the empty frames to the locker.

"Pathetic," she sighs to herself.

So the old goat has heard me then, has he, on those long nights when I've leaned out the nursery window, calling for the Rebbe?

"I should never have taken you in," he mutters now, peering ner-

vously through the open door, across the courtyard, at the nursery window.

"Pan Skibelski is dead!" she shouts at him. "They shot him years ago! His children are dead! His wife is dead! The Jews are dead, they're dead, Uncle! You know this! Everyone knows this! Now if you don't shut up, I'll have Misha put a bullet through your fat head and you'll be dead as well!"

16

I run from the garage to the main apartment, tears stinging my good eye, and rush blindly up the stairs to Ola's room.

"Ola! Ola! I must talk to you at once," I shout, barging through her door.

"Pani Chaim," she says, turning, with a wide smile. "Look at me."

Something about her leaves me, for a moment, unable to speak. She is changed, that is certain, although I can't quite tell how. I stop at her threshold, nearly dropping the framed family portrait, and think to put it on the dresser and then hold it instead, tucked beneath my arm.

"Ola, but what has happened?"

She rushes to me, clasping my hands to her chest.

"I died," she says, merrily.

"You did *what?*" I find her impossible to understand.

"I'm dead," she repeats.

"You died? Ola? But no! When?"

"Minutes ago," she laughs, covering her mouth with her fingers. "Isn't it wonderful?"

With a lightness I have never seen, she pulls on new traveling clothes: a high-waisted skirt, a silk blouse with buttons to the side, a smart tweed frock.

"I no longer need my glasses," she says. And it's true. She moves easily about the room without them, finding her brushes and her combs, which she packs into a small valise.

"Your mother," I say. "Shouldn't someone tell your mother?"

"What happens now?" she asks, all dressed, as if for a sea voyage.

"Ola," I say, but I'm unable to think clearly. Can this really be my Ola, my worn little tubercular Ola, who stands before me with such bright and gleaming eyes? She, too, seems years older than when I saw her last. Was it really only a night ago? How many years has she been living in my house?

"But you said you had something to ask me," she giggles.

As I start to speak, a great rumbling fills the air, clipping my words, interrupting them completely. We rush to the window, Ola and I, towards the source of this monstrous sound. A thundering billow of clouds rises darkly from behind the ancient monastery, blocking the sun. As it does, the clouds are shot through with a light that is astonishingly bright, yet we are able to look at it directly, stare at it even, without its burning our eyes. Somewhere, there is music, a jubilant choir of

voices. I feel queasy in the pit of my stomach. From the center of the clouds, a blue chariot bursts forth, guided by four fiery horses, each with a lion's head and wings that span the sky. A small bearded man with a rounded tummy and long curling peyes sits besides his doting mother.

"Oh, look!" Ola shouts, tears in her eyes. "It's Jesus and Mary!" She no longer shelters her thin body against my bulkier frame, but hangs out the window, gawking.

"Surely not!" I exclaim. That fat mama's boy with the scraggly beard and the blotchy red face? This nebbish is their god?

"But who else could it be, Pani Chaim?"

The stern-looking woman motions benevolently to Ola, beckoning to her with strong arms wrapped in flowing silken sleeves. The son tries his best to control the horses or whatever they are, but they leap and snort and prance against the floor of clouds.

Ola leaves my gripping hands and balances on the window sill. She steadies herself, grasping the edge of the fading blue shutters. Her shoe becomes tangled in the curtain and she nearly falls.

"Easy, easy," the woman calls to her.

Looking down, Ola raises a finger, as if to say, "I'll be fine in a minute, give me a minute."

"Ola, stop this," I whisper. "This is madness."

But she lifts both her arms and closes her eyes and ascends through the sky towards the fiery chariot. Her long skirt billows out and I blush to see her underthings.

"Ola," I shout after her. "Your bag!"

I lift the small valise she had only moments before packed so carefully, containing her few possessions, and the compass and the telescope.

"I don't think I'll be needing it," she calls back with a hapless shrug.

I watch as the bearded man offers her his chubby hand and guides her into the chariot, where she is received with warm kisses from the matronly woman. The three are seated and turn, one last time, to wave at me.

"Goodbye! Goodbye, Pani Chaim!" Ola cups two hands around her mouth to shout this farewell, then she sits back, squirming happily in her seat.

"Shalom aleichem, Reb Chaim!" the matron calls to me.

With difficulty, the man with the scant beard turns the leonine horses towards the monastery, clutching at his yarmulke to keep it from flying off. Small, winged babies pull at the light-filled clouds, closing them like a curtain. The chariot and its angelic retinue disappear behind the monastery roof and are soon gone beyond our wooded horizon. The sky returns to its normal light. The music disappears. From the west, dark clouds roll in and a heavy rain begins.

I look down at my hands and see that, like a fool, I'm still clutching onto my family portrait. I had forgotten all about it. With a handkerchief, I wipe a bit of motor oil from its glass. Behind me, suddenly, there is a shrieking. I turn to find Ola's mother wailing over the waxen corpse that lies like a stick figure in her bed. The woman beats her enormous breasts, pulls at her coarse grey hair.

Tears build up behind the golden rims of her eyeglasses. These she eventually must remove, allowing the dammed waters to flood across her apple cheeks in little curling streams.

"My baby!" she wails. "My Ola!"

I notice that she is wearing Ester's good Sabbath dress and the small cameo I bought for her on a business trip one year to Lodz. I peer into her face, trying to discern from it how much time has passed, but its features are too distorted in their agony for that.

A chorus of hands reach out to the Mama from behind, rubbing her shoulders, patting her head. These belong to her family, but she shakes them off fiercely. More relatives crowd into the room, nearly thirty of them. They stand close to the bed, in a thickening knot, like a group waiting for a tram.

"Get them out!" the Mama shrieks. "Out! I can't breathe!" She throws her heavy body onto the thin corpse of her daughter.

"There, there," Big Andrzej consoles his wife, punching her lightly on the arm. "Your Ola is with her Jesus now."

17

I'm drunk, reeling. They're all at the funeral. I've unlocked the liquor cabinet and gone through the bottles they've stashed there. Two bottles of potato vodka, one of rye whiskey, one of some sticky sacramental wine. Since I'm not able to drink, instead I

relax my tongue and my throat and pour the bitter potions down my gullet. Perhaps I'm drunk only from memory, from the smells. Perhaps I'm not drunk at all. They'll come home and find the empty bottles rolling around on the floor, in any case. Let them. I don't care! Have I really been abandoned twice? First by the Rebbe, and now by Ola! Oh, but the misery of watching her ascend to the Heavens in a fiery chariot, accompanied by her false gods, those idolatrous abominations, while our God, the One True God, has left me neglected here below, answering my pleas with His stony, implacable silence!

The mourners have returned. They sit in the parlor, sighing and weeping, groaning, sutured up so tightly in their shiny black clothes that they can barely breathe. Every now and then, one of them mentions the name *Ola* or the name *Paulina*. It strikes my ear like a savage insult or a bitter taunt. Their pious little daughter, too good for this harsh world. Well, whose daughter is not! I cannot bear their insipid complacencies another minute. Even now, see how they stretch and yawn, scratching their rumbling bellies before marching off to the dining room, like sleepwalkers. If it weren't for their intestines, they wouldn't even know they're alive.

Neighbors, from the old Kaminski and Goldfaden apartments across the courtyard, have prepared a banquet, a feast. Tureens of chlodnik and kapuśniak and sauerkraut soup, pitchers of clabbered milk, boiled potatoes with skwarki, plates of moonshaped pierogi

piled high near plates of pieroźki filled with calf brains near plates of kolduny filled with rabbit meat. There are deep bowls of kasha and uszka and plump rolls of coulibiac. A platter here of salted herring with pickled eggs and one there for a roasted pork shoulder with baked apples and potatoes. Someone has poached a carp in a caramelized raisin sauce. There are cabbages with potatoes and couscous, fiery kielbasa and knackwurst, and a fragrant bigos stew. The scent of juniper berries carries all the way down the street! Roasted squab, shashlik, and a cabbage-smothered pheasant are draped across platters along with a rare stuffed goose. For dessert, there are little mountains of sour-cream blinis, great wheels of red Russian kiśiel, twisted sticks of chrust, golden-brown racuszki sprinkled with confectioners' sugar, raisin-filled babka and a tower of flat piernik cakes.

The sideboard resembles a butcher's window, the serving table a baker's shop. Dazed, in polite couples, the many mourners approach the feast, muttering guiltily about life and its irrefutable demands, about the high importance of living, about how Ola, dear lamb, would have wanted them to live, how she would have wanted them to forget all about her, if need be, in order to continue living, to continue filling their bellies and sucking in air, as though there were not enough of it to go around, as though certain lungs must surrender their portion in order that pinker, more fortunate lungs might expand to full capacity! How they sigh and heave, these fatuous dreamers, flaunting the very air in their chests. Their exhala-

tions fill my nostrils with a putrid stench. Oh, the living, how they stink! They stink! They do! They rot but do not decompose. And each day, these walking, stinking, breathing monsters devour whole forests of animals, entire oceans of fish, great farms of vegetables and to what end? That they may shit and fart and piss their way through another day of violence and indifference. Well, let them pass their lives as someone else's uninvited guests. I want them out! Now! Out of my house!

I enter the dining room and circle the table. With bowed heads, they've finished saying their prayers. "In Jesus' name," they pray, "Amen," praying through the failed rabbinical student they imagine to be God, to the true God, a God they do not know, a God Who hates me, true, it's true, Who hid my fate from me these many years, when I was rich and felt myself so blessed. This is what You had in store for me? To watch helplessly as a family of Polish pigs sits at my table and feeds itself, as though around a trough, snuffling down the delicacies they've stolen from the cellars of my murdered neighbors!

I'll have no more of it.

Big Papa Andrzej has now stood, so solemnly, to thank all his neighbors for their considerable charities. Piously, he motions to his mourning wife, offering up her thanks as well. He is drunk. Like me. Like me, he's been drinking since sun up. His wife, that fat horse of a woman, sobs and sniffs at every mention of her poor daughter's name.

"Ola, Ola, Ola!" I bellow it into her head, not an inch away, so close I can see the stiff hairs growing like foliage inside her plump apricot ears. And out her nose as well. I've peeked around the corner of her head for a better look. There's one curling white hair growing from a wart upon her chin.

The eldest brother rises, also, to offer a toast of thanks to their helpful friends, usurpers of *my* helpful friends and their houses and their homes.

"While you offer up thanks, why not thank your stars that your true landlords are dead in a pit five versts out of town!" I scream, adding to the silence.

Now all the thanks have been offered and the meal continues. As the Papa sits, I can't help it, I pull his chair out from under him. A childish prank, I know, but satisfying nonetheless. He tumbles onto the floor, a look of helpless confusion on his face. But because the family is long used to his drunken misjudgments, they show only the slightest concern, helping him to his feet, until I throw the chair across the room. It shatters against my mother-in-law's mirror, which she gave Ester and me as a wedding gift. The little group of mourners gasps. They cross themselves, leaving their legs unprotected. I take the opportunity to dash around the table, spilling first this plate, then that, onto their open laps. Down the line I go, one after the next. They stand, the food dropping off like clots of mud from their skirts and pants.

I'm on the table now, above their heads, dancing. With every

kick of my feet, I send a tea cup sailing to the right and to the left. They crash and crack against the walls with the light, tinkling sound of someone noodling on a piano. Lifting a platter, I rain squab down upon their heads.

"It's Ola's ghost!" someone screams, raising a protective arm. But why would Ola haunt this house? Her greatest wish, when alive, was to flee it.

"No," says the Papa, sniffing the air. "It's that crazy yid who used to live here. I can smell him."

I have jumped to the floor and am about to rip the curtains from their rods, when the drunken old fool leaps upon the table and does a little mazurka of his own, sending forks and knives scattering in all directions.

"Get down, Andrzej!" the Mama screams.

"Look! Look at me!" he sings out. "I'm a dead yid. I'm the ghost of that Jewish yid!" He contorts his face into twisted poses suggestive, I imagine, of my presumed agony. He yodels spookily, like a man whose throat has just been slashed.

Infuriated, I fling whole drawers of silverware from the sideboard at him. They spill over him, each drawer a small cloudburst of silver rain.

"Aha!" he calls, ducking. "I've got him angry now!"

In retaliation, he kicks the goose from its platter, sends it flying, once again, across the room.

"Here," he says, taking wads of bank notes from an inner pocket of

his vest. "I'll buy the house from you, you christkilling yid! Money, that's all you care about! If that's what you want, well, here it is!" And he throws the bills about the room, in loose fistfuls. "If that's what you want, I'll buy the house from you! Pan Skibelski, can you hear me!"

Everyone is laughing and applauding him, as he chases round the table. The strain of this sight, however, proves too much for the Mama and she is escorted from the room by two of her daughters. They fill up the doorway, three black ravens clucking their tongues, and disappear into another room.

The old father continues capering on the table, ringed by the bright shiny faces of children and cousins and neighbors all about him on the floor.

"Who are you, Andrzej?" they scream up at him.

"I'm the yid!" he shouts back. "I'm the dead yid!" He leans down, pretending to snatch at them with trembling fingers. "Careful or I'll seduce you in the night!"

My heart sinks and the bleeding begins. I'm unable to stand, blood streaming from my eyes and ears, out my anus and my chest. I vomit up whole quarts and sit shaken in a corner.

"Who are you, Uncle Andrzej?" the children call to him.

"I'm Pan Skibelski!" he shouts back.

The room is littered with broken plates and food.

Janek from next door brings in another cache of his homemade vodka. The mourners, even the children, *everyone!* helps himself to another drink. Loud music blares from the phonograph. I pant,

breathlessly, holding my belly, blood filling my clothes, soaking through, stranding me in a large and growing puddle.

The old father continues dancing, to the general delight, across the tabletop. His hat has flown off and his face is puffy and red. Perspiration flies from each of his black and grey hairs. His voice is growing hoarse. "Look at me! Look at me!" he calls. "I'm the dead yid! Careful or I'll seduce you in the night!"

18

I barely stumble up the staircase, clinging to the walls, my sight dimming. Using my hands to steady myself, I find my way to the bathroom and lie there in the rounded tub, tears mingling with the blood dripping from my eye. They trail across my face, stinging my raw and wounded cheek. My legs are splayed and my shoes stick out over the rims. The blood drips back through my socks and runs inside my pant legs and up my thighs.

I am losing consciousness. My arms grapple the sides of the tub, my fingers numbing to their task. I will not be able to hold myself up much longer. For a moment I am terrified I will fall asleep and drown in my own blood. But that is ridiculous. I am already dead. The thought is absurd: a dead man drowning. I laugh quietly and, perhaps because of the awkward position of my body in the tub, some air may have gotten trapped inside my lungs. A

small splash of blood explodes from my nose, staining my collar, my shirtfront and my tie.

WHEN I AWAKEN, my head is pounding, my throat is parched, my eyes burn against a harsh and yellow light.

A candle stands near the sink in a small monument of its own melted wax.

Everything is familiar. The red wallpaper, the unbolted door, the brass faucets. Am I really still *here*? A dull throb pounds behind my forehead. My eye traces a line of pain, following an enormous shadow as it skates across the corners of the wall. The Angel of Death! At last, at last. I attempt to rise, to greet him, to offer my neck for his sword.

WHEN I AWAKEN again, I notice that I am naked.

"Rebbe," my eyes focusing. "Is that really you? Are you really back?"

"I'm back," he screeches. "Of course I'm back. What did you think?" He hops about on the edges of the tub, swooping down to plug the stopper into the drain, the brass chain dangling from his beak.

"Rebbe," I roar out my heart's lament. "Why am I not dead!" I can't help speaking so freely. The sight of him, walking on the lip of the tub, has broken a dam within my heart. I lie back, too weak to move or stand or even sit up for very long.

The Rebbe fills the tub with tepid water, turning the faucets with his beak.

His feathers bristle and he scolds me. "What do you even know about it that you think it should be different? From where do you get such expectations!"

"But how could you just leave me?"

"Chaim, you didn't get my note?"

"Your note!" I say. "Yes, I got your note. Only how could I read it, scrawled in that pigeon scratch, you shouldn't be offended."

"Chaimka," the jaw of his beak slackens. "That was Yiddish."

"Yiddish?" I say. Impossible!

The water rises in the tub, seeping through my bullet holes, filling the hollows of my body with its creeping warmth. The Rebbe flaps his wings and remains stationary, for a moment, in the air.

I close my eyes and wait for the water to reach my ears.

19

The pinkish water drains, in a small swirl, from the tub. The Rebbe carries over a cloth in his beak, one of the towels Ola and I used. I suffer a moment of confusing embarrassment.

He eyes me sharply.

"Rebbe," I stammer in explanation.

"Wash your face now, Chaimka," he says. "There's blood all over it."

How much does he know? Everything, I suspect.

I douse the cloth in the water and bring it to my face, rubbing the cakes of clotted blood from my chin and the crevices of my cheeks.

I stand and the water plashes from the holes in my body like streams from a fountain. The Rebbe wraps me in an enormous towel that is toasty and warm. It smells like Sabbath bread and soon I am dried.

"Gather your things, Chaimka," the Rebbe announces in his piercing squawk. He fluffs up the feathers around his neck. "We leave immediately."

THE COLOR OF POISON BERRIES

20

The sun finally rises, staining the drifts of snow a salmon pink, the color of poison berries. The Rebbe circles overhead. I grab my winter coat and my rustic traveling sack, and off we go, out the courtyard and onto Noniewicza Street, deserted now in the early hours of this freezing winter day. The houses blindly witness our leavetaking through windows layered in icy sheets, their sills and eaves frosted with pale drifts. I clap my hands together for warmth and search through my pockets for my woolen gloves and a

thick woolen scarf. Gifts from my Ester, she knitted them one summer when the doctor forbade her to leave her bed. Which child she was carrying, I can't recall, but it was a difficult, an impossible confinement.

High above, the Rebbe turns in a great wheel, leaving Noniewicza Street to soar above a crooked alleyway. I hesitate to follow him, glancing one last time towards the facade of my court, my shoes sinking into the snow. How small it appears from this distance, a flat rectangular box, no larger than a coffin. I walked through it, not an hour ago, but surely for the final time, its hallways creaking, its walls breathing softly, seeing it not as it is now, filled to the rafters with drowsing Poles, stacked high in their beds like cords of wood, but as it was then, years and years and years ago, when I first stepped foot into it. A bright and clear morning, that was. The builders had only just completed their work. I had commissioned the entire court, with its apartments and its storefronts to rent, saving the largest apartment for ourselves. I snuck in early to hang mezuzahs on the doorposts, to secure a blessing for the house. Every room was empty and expectant. *Here*, I thought, *we will live.*

Not more than an hour ago, before the sun was up, I removed the leather traveling sack from the closet near the front entryway and strapped it across my chest, like a rustic. I hesitated, not knowing what to carry with me. A thought occurs and I step, first in one direction, then in the next, until remembering the photos

hidden in my jacket. These, I secure in a pocket of the bag. I worried that the blood might have ruined them, but they dried out quite nicely. Wrinkled, yes, a little frayed about the edges, but no worse, really, for the wear.

In Ola's room, I kneel against the bed, careful not to awaken her cousins who have claimed it. They sleep, the three of them, embedded in the mattress as deeply as the lice. Running my hand across the floor, I find in the valise beneath her bed, the toy compass and the broken spyglass, which she had so prized. I place them also into the sack. In the kitchen, I steal a loaf of raisin bread, left over from the mourners' feast, to make a surprise banquet for the Rebbe. Fending for himself, he has surely grown weary of the seeds and worms and other staples of an avian diet. I wrap the bread in paper and, tucking it into the traveling sack, I remember the ledger book hidden in my office across the courtyard. So out the door and into the brisk dark morning, past the timberyard and bare gardens, to the big warehouse. Following its ramp into my office, I dig with my hand into the cushions of the daybed, finding nothing. I ransack the drawers of my desk, scattering their contents, tossing them wildly about, but the ledger isn't there. A feeling of panic floods my nerves. I kick myself. I should have known better than to leave important documents lying about! I'm forgetting everything!

Utterly dejected, I sit at the desk and notice how unpleasant the cushions feel. Of course! I had hidden the ledger inside the cushion

of my chair. At the time, I recall, it seemed the only place. Why? I no longer have any idea.

The Rebbe squawks and I must hurry to catch up with him. I have been daydreaming. We are already outside the Jewish quarter. I'm trailing a thin line of blood in the snow, but otherwise, I feel up to the journey, if a little creaky and stiff in the joints.

The town disappears behind us. *You'll never be back,* a voice whispers in my ear. I march beneath a thick mesh of trees. *Never, never, never.* I sing a little traveling song, to cheer myself. The Rebbe sails overhead on a nearly silent wind.

A thatch of snow grows too heavy for the tree branch supporting it. It breaks and falls with a loud and wooden crack.

2 1

Our first stop is the pit of buried Jews. How different the place appears in winter, so quiet and so still. It's difficult even to find the raised mound beneath its many thick quilts of snow.

"Rebbe," I call up. "If I'm not mistaken, here is where they killed us."

Although it's difficult to tell.

The day is gleaming with the sun reflected everywhere in the bright clean snow.

The Rebbe stretches his wings and glides easily to the ground.

He lands with such grace, you'd think he'd been a crow his entire life. Because he is light, he doesn't sink in, like me, but skates across the ivory surface of the drifts, leaving two lines of arrow-shaped clawprints as a trail. His small head bobs rhythmically forward and back, forward and back, in a black blur, and he hunts and pecks through the drifts, searching out our hidden grave.

I watch quietly. I know better than to interrupt him when his concentration is so fierce.

Often, at shul, when his prayers grew especially fervent, those of us near to him had to move away. Otherwise, we might have burned up, God forbid, in the holy fires that surrounded him.

He leaps into the air.

Flying low to the ground, the Rebbe circles the perimeter of the grave seven times, wheeling to the right, then wheeling three times to the left. He screeches out odd phrases of Hebrew and Aramaic, phrases I have never heard uttered in this fashion, nor in this order, and never in a voice so metallic and strange.

I sense a slight trembling beneath my shoes, and soon the earth is shaking madly below my feet. Blocks of shining snowdrifts rise up, as if pushed, and crumble all about. I grab onto a branch to steady myself and accidentally bite my tongue.

"Rebbe!" I shout, spitting out lines of bloody saliva. "The ground is churning!"

But I have lost sight of him.

The air erupts with an agonized groan. I have to cover my ears

with my hands, so terrible are its cries. I cower, on one knee, behind a birch tree. Above me, I can hear the Rebbe's squawking among the mad chatterings of birds as they depart from their nests in frantic numbers.

With a great ripping, the ground splits open like an old pair of trousers.

Inside the circle described by the Rebbe's flight, first the snow and then the frozen dirt sinks in and falls upon itself, like white and brown sugar being sifted in an enormous baker's bowl. Puffs of silt rise into the cold air, as though someone had dropped an open sack of flour. The entire world disappears.

"Rebbe?" I say, coughing. "I can't see anything!"

From nowhere, the Rebbe lands upon my shoulder with such force, he nearly knocks me on my face.

I clutch at my troubled back, trying to straighten up. "Be careful, Rebbe, can't you!" I say, surprised, and alarming myself with my pique.

He crows, "Well, Chaimka?" puffing up his little chest and seems to arch an eyebrow, although I know that cannot be. He has none. Still, he gestures me forward with his wing.

I hoist myself up on my cane and, not without qualms, hobble nearer to the lip of the opened grave. Through the grey and white marblings of clouds, the sky lets down dusty shafts of light. I wave a handkerchief in front of us, attempting to see through the thick-

ened, grainy air. Moving my feet without lifting them, I probe the ground with the rubber tip of my stick, searching for the drop.

By degrees, the dust settles, and small faces begin to appear behind its thinning veils. The Rebbe and I stand above them at the edge of the decline. Arms raised to block the day's brightness, they bend their necks to look at us, thousands of ragged men and women, their dark-circled eyes blinking against the too-dazzling light. What a curious sight we must make, a tall, heavy man in a dark suit with a black crow perched upon his shoulder. But no less curious are they! Although the harsh winter seems to have slowed their decay, their milk-white bodies show evidence not only of rot, but also of mutilation. I recognize a face or two. It isn't easy. The soldiers' lime has eaten into their skins, gnawing deep rouged gashes into their chins, into their cheeks. Their arms, raised, leave black shadows slanting across their pale, disastrous features.

But certainly there's Reb Yudel the candlemaker. We nod to each other, a silent greeting, and I see that he's missing an arm.

With a dirty hand, Basha Rosenthal wipes a tear from a lost eye. Her child plays at her broken feet, without its jaw.

Rivke Siedenberg, my old seductress, bravely holds her disemboweled viscera in with two unsteady arms.

A man I can no longer identify uses two pincer-like fingers to delicately extract a worm from the cavity in his blackened cheek. He pulls and pulls at its slithering tail, curling it in loops around his little finger.

"Reb Chaim!" he waves an arm at me. "Greetings!"

My stomach heaves into my throat. I whistle through my teeth, sickened by the stench. I bring a handkerchief to my nose and attempt to nod in reply.

The Rebbe leaves my shoulder and lands upon the arm of a thin man whose greenish skin shows through the tatters in his suit.

"Rebbe?" the man squints through the thick rheum covering his eyes. "Is it really you?"

Joy splits his cracked lips. His teeth are yellow and broken. Those near to him crowd in to be closer to the Rebbe. The greenish man raises the Rebbe, in two hands, for all to see.

"Ah," he happily drools. "What a wonderful world indeed!"

2 2

I reach down, bending on my knees, and offer my hand to Reb Elimelech. He scrambles up the side, clinging to my lowered arm. On his feet now, he brushes a colorless hand through the tangles of his long and silvery beard, combing crumbly balls of dirt and frantic insects from inside it. We look into each other's unbelieving faces, our hands clamping onto each other's arms, and soon we are hugging and weeping and laughing all at once, although, pressed in against his chest, I can't help noticing how rotten and decomposed he smells!

I struggle to escape his grip, but it's useless. He's too excited to see me.

"Will you look at you, old friend!" he shouts, his arms around me like a vise. "Chaimka!" Mercifully, he holds me now at arm's length for a better look, grunting. "So they shot you in the back of the head, did they?"

I choke out the words, "Yes, and through my belly and chest as well." I slip away from him and stand at a distance, as if to demonstrate my wounds. But even at this remove, his stench is overpowering. "Later," I say, "in private, I'll show you the holes."

He nods, grimly.

"And you, Reb Elimelech?"

"Through the heart, I think," he probes a nervous hand into his sunken breast. "I'm not certain. It's been so dark, I couldn't check."

All about us, the prisoners have shaken off their lethargy. Prayers are whispered, thanks is loudly offered up. Their confusing freedom overtakes them in its rush. Everyone tries to climb out of the grave at once. Children scramble up its uneven slopes, against their parents' wishes. A rope is fashioned out of shirts and pants, and various ones fight to be the first to climb it.

"One at a time!" "Out of my way!" "Stop pushing, you!"

Holding on to Reb Elimelech's sleeve, I search the crowd, looking past unfamiliar faces for more familiar ones.

"So Chaim," Reb Zundel slaps me on the back, "where have you been hiding?"

"How are Ester and the children?"

"Did you look into those trolley fares?"

Fruma Leibe asks the first question, brushing mud from the knees of her long skirt, Reb Elchonon and Reb Mendele the second, standing before me, arm in arm.

Hopping mad, Reb Zev Wolf gives chase to a young boy who has run off with his severed foot. Reb Elimelech's eyes crinkle. He can't help laughing, and neither can the rest of our little group.

"Ah, what a morning," he says, and we all sigh with sadness and relief.

But soon the dead Jews begin to shiver. Their ragged, infested garments offer little warmth against the cold. Many are barefoot and must leap from foot to foot to keep their toes from freezing.

"I told you to keep track of your socks, Yankel, but do you listen?" a mother berates her child, who runs from her in tears.

Despite these discomforts, we gibber-jabber happily, everybody catching up on everybody else's tale. The sun sows its light, like seeds, into the snow. The day feels like Tashlich, when, at the new year, we'd walk, the entire town, to the river to cast our sins into its accepting waters. Of course, today, we'd only find it frozen.

I sigh and look about.

Did they really have to kill us all?

A sharp whistle pierces the din, and we are silenced. Raising my eyes, I locate the Rebbe high on the branch of a frosted larch. He swoops through the air, circling and descending, landing finally on my shoulder, again with surprising force.

"Time to leave, Chaimka," he pipes into my ear.

Digging his claws into my coat, he springs up and is aloft, turning south in a wheeling arc.

"Landsmen!" I shout, cupping my hands about my mouth. "We are heading south! Stay together, be of good cheer, assist one another, and with the help of God, we will all see each other there in a few short days."

I tie a blood-soaked handkerchief to the end of my walking stick, holding it up like a flag for everyone to follow. We trudge off, Reb Elimelech and myself in the lead, the little town of Jews behind us, each one trailing his own thin trickle of blood. If you were the Rebbe, floating high above us, what you would see would be a great river of blood cutting a swath through the frozen winter hills.

23

"Is it true?" Reb Elimelech asks, marching beside me.

"Is what true?" I say.

He lowers his voice. "What we heard about the moon?"

I'm exasperated.

"Do I have the moon?" I say. "Do you have the moon? No, but still, we're all thieves! We're all to blame!"

"Well," Reb Elimelech hugs himself tighter, trying not to shiver. "Surely, it's behind us now."

"What exactly is behind us now?" I ask.

"Everything," he says. "For where else could the Rebbe be leading us, if not to the World to Come?"

The World to Come, the World to Come.

I grunt, hoping he is right, and look past him at the sunset, spreading like a purple bruise behind the hills.

WE SLEEP THAT night, as best we can, near a quiet wheat field. Exhausted, shivering, the Jews have no choice but to lie upon the hard and frozen ground. This, of course, inspires many new and several old complaints. The Zionists and the Bundists have banded together and are demanding blankets for everyone. From where we are to procure these, no one knows. Members of the Mizrachi group are refusing to sleep anywhere near members of the Agudas. Even dead, their bitter disagreements continue unresolved. The Communists have made their own camp, "scientifically selected," near a ragged fence. Anyone who wants is invited to join them there. As a result, most of the older Jews have scurried like frightened mice across the field, so as to be nowhere near them. A group of women are grumbling already of how they miss their grave, so secure and warm were they beneath the earth.

"Of course, it was dark, with all sorts of horrors, but at least we were together, without this constant bickering."

"We had bickering in the pit," her companion dares to contradict her.

"We had no bickering."

"We had plenty of bickering!"

"Such nonsense!"

"You don't know what you're talking about."

"All right, so we had bickering, but at least it wasn't petty."

"It was petty."

"All right, it was petty, but at least we knew where we would sleep each night."

Small cells of resisters have sprung up, defiant men clustering in tense groups around distant trees. Their arms are crossed and their eyes are shifty and private. Fretting, they mutter and make speeches to each other.

I pass near enough to hear their words, clumsy with emotion.

"Consider the facts," says one, a young firebrand, still muscular despite his time beneath the ground.

"And what are the facts?"

His eyes shine as he answers the men gathering before him.

"For one thing," he says, "we're moving around."

"True," the others have to concede.

"We're speaking to each other."

"It's a good point," the group turns in upon itself, mumbling, muttering.

"We're all still bleeding."

"It never stops, that's true!" they cry.

"So perhaps . . ."

"Perhaps what?" Moyshe Leib the tailor steps forward. "Perhaps we haven't died?" he asks incredulously.

"I feel we should at least consider the possibility. Or cease to call ourselves men!" The young hothead makes one last attempt to arouse the passions of the others.

"Reb Dovid, you were in a pit underneath the ground for how long?" his antagonist counters, not unkindly.

"True," Reb Dovid lowers his eyes, searching the ground pointlessly.

"With no air."

"No, it's true," he is defeated, his arguments frustrated.

"Without food or water."

"I know, I know. You think I didn't notice!"

"Perhaps we haven't died, you say? Perhaps we were never alive in the first place!"

"But why are we not in the World to Come?"

The World to Come, the World to Come.

They chant these words like starving workers demanding bread from a government storehouse. And like a snake, the anguished phrase slithers away from them and into the larger group, biting an ankle here, an ankle there, until everyone is infected by the poison of its doubt.

A cache of dirty blankets appears from nowhere in an old abandoned shed. The Rebbe's doing, I feel certain. The people fight over

the wretched strips of cloth and cover themselves as best they can. They've put sleep off as long as possible but are now unable to resist its pull. Groaning, they sink into the snow. Mothers hug their children, husbands press against their wives, brothers huddle near brothers, hoping to warm themselves in the bitter whistling wind. I'm reminded of a typing pool, so many teeth are chattering.

I pull my coat tighter about myself. I cannot sleep among them, so powerful is their stench. A moldy humic tang. They all stink of it and no amount of washing in the snow seems able to relieve them of its fetid odors. Apparently, they don't smell it on each other, and although I've passed the better part of the day in their company, I've yet to grow accustomed to it, and am undone, often to the point of a swimming nausea, if I linger too long or too near.

24

They lie lifelessly in the snow, three thousand bundles dropped by a careless traveler. They sleep, their bickering unresolved. They are frightened, of course. And who can blame them? This afternoon, we walked through a small town, spilling our blood in its narrow streets. Only the children saw us. Most ran away in fright, but many threw rocks and jeered. No one has any idea when our sufferings will end.

I sit upon a poorly cut tree stump. The peasants will use any-

thing, anything at all, to slice down their wood, without concern for next season's forest or its harvest. Enough starlight is reflected in the white fields for me to see the outlines of a figure as it stands at the far end of our pasture. On its knees at first, it pushes itself up by its hands and spins in slow circles, searching for something or someone. Cautiously, it traces a winding route though the maze of ragged bundles, careful not to step upon a leg or an arm or a hand. Its sex is masked by the triangular shape of the blanket that hangs, like a prayer shawl, from its shoulders. It walks slowly, but gradually I realize, in my direction. Its musty smells reach me long before the figure itself, which soon shuffles its feet before me, waiting for my acknowledgment.

I peer through the murk at the outline of its narrow head, at the bottom of which seems to float a luminous white funnel.

"Reb Chaim," the figure clears its throat.

"Reb Elimelech?" I say, squinting uselessly through the gloom.

"I was hoping to have a word."

"Of course, my friend, of course." I make a space for him beside me on the ice-hardened stump. "Sit, please, do."

He sits and seems to nod amiably, although it's too dark really to see more than the white triangular beard against the dark fabric of his blanket, the occasional reflection of snow glimmering in the pupils of his eyes.

He pulls the blanket closer to his chest, clasping its hems to-

gether in his fist. I wait, but he says nothing and clears his throat again.

"Please," I say. "Feel free to speak your mind."

I know him only too well. He will require at least a second invitation and possibly a third before permitting himself to speak.

He kicks with his foot at the snow.

"Reb Chaim," he says, "forgive me. I've been tossing and turning all night, unable to sleep. Certain unpleasant thoughts won't leave me. However, I have no wish to disturb you with them."

"I assure you, you're not."

"Then permit me to ask: how long have we known one another?"

"Forever," I say. "Since we were boys."

We'd sit in cheder, our heads pressed together, learning Mishnah. *Two men hold a garment. One says, This is mine, and the other says, This is mine.*

"Have I not been a friend to you then all these years? Were your affairs not as dear to me as my own? Did your children not call me uncle and think of me, on occasion, as a second father?"

"Of course," I say, shifting my buttock. The stump is growing cold. "You were as dear to me as a brother."

"Did I not seek your counsel and offer you mine in return? When we were sick, did we not cheer each other? Did we not shore each other up in times of sadness or distress?"

"Of course, of course," I say. "You have done all that one man

could for another. You have nothing to rebuke yourself for on my account, if that is what you're wondering."

"Then why did you leave me in the pit?"

I am startled by his question. "Pardon me?" I say.

"I must know."

"Is this an accusation?"

"You just ran, didn't you?"

"I ran. Of course, I ran! What else was I to do?"

"Without thinking to stop or help anybody else!"

"Keep your voice down," I implore him, stealing a look into the sleeping field.

"But how could you just leave us there?"

"You were dead," I whisper.

"But so were you!" he shouts.

"What did you expect me to do?"

The blanket falls from his shoulders. The black outlines of his arms shake furiously.

"Didn't you hear me calling? Why didn't you look? Didn't you even look!"

I stammer, seeing before me, in the tangled pile of bodies, an open screaming mouth.

"Yes," I say. "Once. Quickly."

"But you didn't stop, did you!" He fumbles for his blanket, bending at the waist.

"I'd been shot in the head," I scream. "I wasn't thinking clearly!"

. . .

I TRY TO sleep, standing, inside a hollow tree. The ruined trunk provides enough of a barrier to keep the wind from whistling through my head wound. *Why did I not help anyone on the day we were shot?* The thought never even occurred to me! And now it won't go away. It curses my sleep. All night long, whenever I'm able to nod off, it returns. *How could I just leave them?* I stick my head out of the large knothole and search for a glimpse of the Rebbe's nest. The tree line stands in silhouette against the deep lavender sky. He could be sleeping anywhere in the trees or among the bodies lying in the snow. If only he were here, inside my vest, nestled against my heart, then maybe I could sleep.

I reach into my traveling bag and fumble among its contents for the little spyglass. I raise the tube to my eye and, through its fractured lens, search the field for his small, distinctive head.

My heart freezes.

Moving through the sleepers, they jostle the bundles, poking and prodding them with wet and snarling snouts.

Wolves!

I experience a desire to run and feel doubly ashamed for it.

I am frantically searching through my mind for the correct course of action, when one of the wolves raises up on its hind legs.

"Chaim Skibelski!" it seems to cry in a long and mournful whine.

The others wolves stop shifting. They lift their ears and listen. I watch them through my telescope, making as little noise as possi-

ble. A nervous wind blows across the field, stirring the barren trees.

Is it possible a wolf has howled my name?

I tremble inside my tree trunk, my scrotum tightening inside my pants.

"Chaim Skibelski!" the wolf repeats his doleful wail, nose raised and sniffing. I can't tell if he is larger than the others or just nearer to me, the night is so thick. His green eyes glint in flashes as they sweep across the field. *Hunger,* this curious word pounds inside my brain.

"What do you want?" I say, bending so my face is level with the knothole. "There's no point in waking everyone!"

The wolf stands still, his ears twitching, one paw raised.

"Is that really you, Reb Chaim?" he calls out, his breath steaming in the air.

"I am here," I say, poking my head from the tree. Instantly, the wind whips through my head wound with a searing electrical pain, an icy current singes the inside of my skull. Worse than the worst of toothaches. "What do you want?" I cry, unintentionally betraying my pain.

The wolf leaps towards my tree and stands, leaning, with his forepaws against the bark of the trunk. The rest of the pack skulks gingerly behind him in a gang. I can hear the tinkle of snow falling in small patches from the undercoat of his belly. His breath is very near. I shrink inside my tree, hiding from his gaze. But he sticks his twitching rictus into the knothole. Shifting his long head back and forth, he searches out my scent. His tongue clacks and the forest is

on him like a stale cologne, a musty tincture of squirrel carcass, pine needles, and juniper berry oil.

He slavers, "Ah, Chaimka," in a voice both cold and sly.

"Who are you?" I ask. My words quaver, despite my efforts to steady them. I press my back as tightly as I can against the inner bark, moving away from his twitching maw.

"You're on our territory," he whines, forcing his snout in deeper through the hole until it blocks my remaining light. His wet tongue licks his teeth. It sounds like the latches of a suitcase being unlatched. His saliva splatters my wrist where it's bared at the cuff and his whiskers bristle smartly against my skin.

I can hear the other wolves snickering, although faintly, muffled by the wooden chamber of my tree.

"But you'll belong here," he says, "when we eat and excrete you into our soil."

The sniggering comes from all directions.

"Who are you?" I repeat. "I demand that you identify yourself."

"You know me," he whines.

I open my eyes wide to peer through the pitch at his lean and hairy face. Is it possible I know him from somewhere before? I'm about to clear my throat to speak, when his snout lunges forward, growling. He nips at my hand. I batten his face with my cane, raising it as high as I can in my constricted space. He yelps, pulling back.

"How dare you threaten us!" I shout, climbing with difficulty from my trunk.

The pack thunders around my tree before disappearing into the darkened woods. Their untamed stench hangs, like a fume, in the air.

I run after them, not knowing what I'm doing or why. I run through the high drifts and into a narrow ravine. Panting, I'm forced to stop. It's impossible to keep up with them.

"Wolves?" I cry out. "Are you there?"

An echo throws these stupid words back into my face. They have tricked me. And now I wait for them to pounce, to tear my dead body into a thousand pieces.

Quickly, I recite the Vidui, as one must before one dies.

Of course, if I am already dead, the prayer may be superfluous.

I drop to my knees and brace myself. The snow moistens my trouser legs.

"Look, wolves!" I shout, throwing away my walking stick. "I have no weapons now! Nothing to beat you back with. Nothing to defend myself!"

But nothing happens and, finally, I must stand and retrieve the stick, which I shake at them in a rage, screaming into the copse.

"I'm not going to wait all night! In the freezing cold!" I shout. And the echo shouts back at me. "If you're going to devour me, devour me now! Or else let's forget the entire thing!"

"Wolves!" I scream, listening for a reply.

The snow begins to fall, with its soft sounds.

"Wolves? Can you hear me?" I say.

But they must have moved off.

"Wolves . . . ?"

25

By the time I return to our camp, limping and frozen, my hand swollen where the wolf has bitten it, there is a red glow low on the horizon. Dawn. A cadre of volunteers moves silently among the sleeping Jews, stirring and shaking them, rousing them gently for morning prayers. I watch as various ones rise and begin to move about, shaking the feeling back into their legs, careful not to damage the morning's fragile silences. Their eyes are bleary with sleep, and they look about, uncertain where they are or even how they came to be here. Some wash their hands in the snow, reciting the blessings softly. Others simply rub a handful into their gashed faces. Attempting to stand on uncertain legs, a woman falls back onto her haunches, stifling a giddy reel of laughter. "Avigdor," she whispers to her sleeping husband. "Come, help me up. We're alive."

The sun slips, like a thief, through a crack in the clouds, tossing a spray of solar diamonds onto the slanting fields.

Wrapping their blankets about them, many of the men begin to

pray. The women pray, in groups, behind them. They whirl and sway, like ghouls, these half-devoured Jews. I watch from a copse of trees, unable to join in. What can God be thinking? I turn away and lean my back against a tree.

It's then that I see him.

My hands instinctively rise above my head. Elevated, the bitten one pulses and throbs with a searing blue pain.

A young soldier points his rifle at my face.

"One step more," he says, "and I'll kill you again."

26

What can God be thinking! This blasphemous thought forces its way back into my head, like an anarchist into the czarina's bedroom. His gun against my spine, the soldier pushes me into the woods and away from the others. My wounded hand, raised high, aches and throbs. It's growing infected, I can tell. I can feel the pus collecting in the piercings of the teethmarks. This, more than anything else, infuriates me. That I should be marched off by some hooligan with unsound morals when my wounds need tending!

"Keep marching, keep marching, that's right," his voice is flat and nasal. It cuts into my nerves like an acid. The circular tip of his gun keeps poking into my back with a bruising indifference. The crunching of his heavy boots in the dry snow is finally more than I can bear.

"All right! Enough foolishness!" I say, turning to face him. Taking its long barrel between both hands, I thrust the other end of his gun against his chest, knocking sharply into him with a hard dull thud. Where I receive the strength to pummel him so brutally, I have no idea. Clenching my fist, with its infected bites, around the cold metal only aggravates my pain, and this increases my fury. I rap the gun butt a few more times into the direct center of his chest, tearing the scabbing off my hand in the process. He struggles to maintain his balance and releases the gun. To my horror, his head topples from his neck and falls, like a melon, at his feet.

How hard have I hit him?

"Now look what you've done, you impudent dog!" the head barks these hateful words at the laces on my shoes.

I menace it with my foot. "Stop talking like that," I say, "or I'll kick you down the hillside!"

Paying no attention to my threat, the head shouts frantic commands to its body—"Over here! Schnell! Schnell!"—but, of course, the body is deaf without its ears. It cannot hear a word. Indeed, it stumbles blindly about, searching on its knees for the lost gun, lashing out with its fists to fend off a slew of imagined aggressors. A wool scarf hangs loosely around the empty pedestal of its neck. With this, I assume, it had wrapped its head into place.

"You stinking yid," the head screams up at me. "I'm giving you an order! Do you understand? Put me back on my body or I'll kill you right now, right now!"

"Enough!" I roar. I've heard enough. Without thinking, I give the head a swift kick and away it goes, rolling down the hill.

"My eyeglasses!" it screams, spinning and cutting a wobbling path through the drifts.

Running to catch up to it, I kick it a few more times and swat it once or twice, for good measure, with the butt of its gun.

"Will the killing never end?" I shout. "Does it not cease, even after we are dead?"

"Ouch! Ow! Stop it! I'm ordering you! You are my prisoner!" it clamors, whenever its mouth, wheeling in its many revolutions, is not muffled by the ground.

"How do you like it, head?" I shout, delivering a few more kicks.

Perhaps because of the pain in my hand, I am unusually severe.

At the base of a small hillock, it stops, and I grab its hair in my fingers and bury its face in the snow.

"I could suffocate you! Do you hear?" I shout this into its ears, grinding its nose against the icy ground. "What is *wrong* with you? They give you a gun and so you think you own the world!"

"Please, Herr Jude," it coughs out small morsels of snow. "I can't see without my glasses."

I lift the head, like a globe, in both hands and hold it at arm's length by the ears, turning it so that I may look at it directly. Ganglia dangle like strands of seaweed from the bottom of its severed neck, but the brow is well formed, and even handsome. A firm, square jaw, dotted by a day's beard. Deep sorrowful eyes, the color

of chocolate. A long straight nose, with two pink triangles, one on either side, where the glasses had ridden.

Carefully licking its bloody lips, the head probes its wounds with its tongue.

It squints into my good eye.

"Please, Herr Jude," it says, "can't you help me find them?"

"Your glasses?" I say.

Raising my eyes, I scan the fields, but all I see is a headless body running like an escaped lunatic through the trees and deep into the woods.

"Oh dear," the head says, squinting in dismay.

27

Carrying him, like a pumpkin, in the crook of my arm, the gun hanging by its strap across my back, I climb the hill, retracing our path, in search of its lost eyeglasses.

"This is very kind of you," he says, all meekness now. "The first time this happened, I was not so fortunate. My body panicked, was running everywhere. Well, you saw for yourself how it reacts. If I hadn't accidentally stumbled over myself, I don't know where I'd be."

"You'd be exactly where you are now," I point out. "No worse, no better off."

"True," it agrees. "Still, before, I had my eyeglasses and so perhaps I didn't feel quite so bad."

It's not many more steps before I hear a soft tinkling underneath the sole of my left shoe.

"Ah, well," he says, trying to conceal his unhappiness.

Balancing the head on my thigh, I bend down and search cautiously with my hand. I lift the spectacles, covered now with scales of transparent snow. One lens is shattered and the golden frame is bent and ruined.

"They were buried," I say.

"Yes," he says tightly.

"I must've stepped on them," I say.

"I realize that," he says. "But straighten them out, if you can. And perhaps they'll not be entirely worthless."

I place the head between two forking tree roots, securing it there.

"Ah-h-h," it says. "The snow is very cold, Herr Jude."

"But I don't know what else to do with you," I say.

"It's perfectly all right." And he smiles gamely, squinting at my hands as they begin to probe and work the metal rims.

"I have an additional pair in my breast pocket," the head won't cease its endless chattering. "They wouldn't allow me into battle otherwise. Without them, I'm as good as blind. I'm hoping you didn't smash those as well when you pummeled me in the chest."

"That wasn't my fault," I say. I can't help growing cross with this

garrulous head. "You should never have poked your gun into my back!"

He smiles grimly. "I'm not prepared to argue the theoretics of warfare here and now with a dead Jew." He spits this last word off his tongue as though it were an annoying scrap of tobacco. "If it weren't for you," he says, "I'd still be at the conservatory, working on my compositions." He stretches his lower lip into a frown.

"If it weren't for me?"

"For your people."

"And what did we have to do with it?"

"Let's just say I've been denied everything, because of you, including a heroic death."

On their own, my hands clench into fists, and a shard of the broken lens pierces my folding palm.

"I tell you this in the strictest confidence," the head continues. "I wasn't killed in battle. No. I died ingloriously. A big peasant snuck up behind me and cut off my head. With an axe." He laughs bitterly. "Lord knows what my family will think, my mother. I barely had time to cry out."

I consider kicking him down the hill again, so tired am I of his blathering.

Instead I say, "Your glasses are beyond repair, I'm afraid."

I conceal from his blurred vision my bleeding palm and the crumpled golden rims, tucking both into my pocket.

"I was afraid of that," he says.

I stand and look to the horizon.

"Well," I say, drying my palms with a handkerchief. "It's been a pleasure knowing you."

"You're not leaving me, are you?"

I sigh.

"I'm completely dependent on you. You know that," he says.

Even his voice sickens me.

"I'm sorry I pointed my gun at you, Herr Jude," he cries, "but the woods are full of wolves."

"Yes, it's true," I say, my hands smarting in my pockets. "How, I'm sure, they'd love to nibble at your ears!"

"Herr Jude, stop it! You're scaring me!" The head rolls around in little circles of fear. "Don't be cruel! It isn't fair of you to take advantage! You mustn't leave me here!"

He looks blindly up at me, squinting past my knees, begging for my help. He's pathetic! I'm certain he'd have me on the ground before him, groveling for my life, given half the chance.

I feel like kicking him in the teeth.

And yet I can't help feeling vaguely sorry for him. Poring over his musical charts, a student, late into the night, certainly he never imagined that the tired head, which he lovingly cradles in the cup of his hands, would one day be thrown about the countryside by an enraged and vengeful Jew. How difficult it must be for him to humble himself and plead.

"All right," I say, lifting him with one hand by the hair.

"That's a little painful, Herr Jude."

I curl my arm around his ear, pressing the other ear against the side of my hip.

"It's difficult for me to hear this way."

I rotate his head, so that both ears are now uncovered.

"Is that better?"

The head shakes itself. "I can't seem to get comfortable."

In its panic, his body left a melee of footprints in the snow. The pattern crosses and recrosses itself so many times that it's virtually impossible to follow.

28

Searching through the fields, we come upon a portion of the trail that branches off into the trees. Although the footprints here remain equally chaotic—here and there, more often than I can count, they lead directly into a heavy solid tree!—one can discern in their looping meanderings the arc of a general direction. And so this is the trail we take, the head and I, moving deeper into the woods.

There is no use in calling out, the body cannot hear us. Surely panic and confusion will exhaust it. Otherwise, I shall never overtake it, old and weary as I am. Its strides are too vigorous and muscular from its military training. Also the head is heavy and I must

continually shift it from arm to arm, in order to sustain its weight. Although these reshiftings slow us down, the head endures them patiently. How else are we to continue? Keeping my hand, like a strap, beneath its chin, I can feel it swallowing periodically. The sensation is unnerving, needless to say, but what am I to do? Carrying it on my shoulder is out of the question. I couldn't bear having it so near. Kicking it along in front of me, although pragmatic, seems needlessly cruel and surely the head would protest. I've left my satchel back in the hollow tree trunk where I slept (was it only a night ago?) before the wolves disturbed me. If only I had thought to snatch it— although why would I have?—the head would now ride in comfort and any time I tired of its rantings, I could close the flap over it, pinning the wooden peg through the leather loop, sealing it in.

Instead, I'm forced to lug it through these woods like an invalid lugging a medicine ball at a spa!

At other times, and at the head's behest, I carry it backwards so that it may observe the trail behind us, in case the body, in its blind stumblings, doubled back, and we have inadvertently passed it.

These winter days are short and, soon, it's impossible to see further and we are forced to give up our search and stop to rest for the night. I lay the head, not gently, on the ground. My arms ache.

"Brrrr," the head's teeth chatter. "It's so very cold!"

"Yes, it's cold," I say, leaning the gun against a tree. "Of course, it's cold." I sit upon the frigid ground.

"You couldn't perhaps hold me on your lap, could you, Herr Jude?"

"On my lap?"

"Because the ground is frozen."

I am tired and cross after so many exertions on the head's behalf and so I refuse.

"You at least have clothes," it persists, whining. "How can I spend all night up to my neck in the snow!"

"You should have thought of that before you joined the army! Before you attacked me!" I turn my back on him.

"Heartless," it mutters. "All of you."

"What was that!" I snap, standing. I point a warning finger at the uneven part in its hair.

It apologizes quickly.

"You apologize," I say. "Of course, you apologize! But only when it's in your advantage to do so! Everything you say is corrupt! I can't stand listening to you any longer." And I move as far away from him as I can.

"Don't leave me here, Herr Jude!" The head rolls after me, knocking into my feet. I nearly trip over him in the fading light.

"I'm frightened!" he shouts these words up at me, spitting snow from his mouth. His hair is wet, from perspiration or from his travels in the frost, it's impossible to tell. He bites into my shoe leather to keep me near, and I am forced to shake him off with a few sharp kicks. He bounces a short distance across the field once or twice before knocking into a rough spruce.

"Was that necessary?" it shrieks.

"You, I'll see in the morning," I say and turn away from him to make my bed against a sheltered oak, but the little sounds of his weeping are more than I can bear.

Standing, I rip the woolen scarf from my neck.

"Such nonsense!" I exclaim.

He sniffs, "Thank you, Herr Jude," as I wrap the scarf in loops around the puckered circle of his neck. "I only hope my body has found someone equally as kind."

"At least you can be certain it hasn't hanged itself from a tree in despair!"

The head is silent for a moment.

"There's no reason to be so cruel."

"Please." I finish tucking it in. "I have no idea why I am helping you. Don't make it worse for me by constantly speaking!"

I'm about to drift off to sleep, when I feel the head nudging against my arm.

"Herr Jude," it whispers, snuggling against me.

"What *now?*" I manage to say through a drowsy veil.

"Are you sleeping, Herr Jude?"

Annoyed, I turn over to peer at it through the darkness. It has rolled next to me, pulling my scarf along in its teeth. Because my head is also on the ground, we are, once again, face to face.

"I couldn't sleep," it says.

"No?" I say.

"I can't get comfortable."

"I'm sorry," I say

"I generally sleep on my stomach," it says.

The stars shine through our canopy of bare trees. The head sighs, rolling back, so that its eyes may search the Heavens.

"As a boy, when I couldn't sleep, my grandfather would take me in his lap," this the head confides to me. "He worked making Mercedes Benzes. I'd sit in his lap, he'd bring me hot cocoa. The smells of the oil and the grease from his work would mingle with the chocolate and the honey." The head sighs. "Ah, what I wouldn't do right now for a cup of hot cocoa!"

"It would run out the bottom of your neck and spill all over the ground," I say, sitting up stiffly and yawning.

29

"Herr Jude," the head whispers to me. Without my realizing it, it has inched its way into my lap, as though it were a child. "I have a story to tell you."

Where, I wonder, are my fellow Jews? Where are they lodging for the night? And what sins have I committed that I am parted from them and must sleep instead with this sentimental murderer, forced to hear tales of its boyhood and its youth?

"Once upon a time," it begins.

And there's no dissuading him.

"We were chasing two Jews through the woods. Not like you, Herr Jude, but the other kind, the funny-looking ones."

I ask him to clarify.

"With the long coats and the funny hats and the corkscrew side-burns sticking out from in front of their ears. It was comical just to see them run, they look so much like penguins."

How painful it is to listen to this head.

"What do you call them?"

How little he knows!

"We had rounded up a whole pack of them, but these two . . . Hasids . . ." he tries the word out for himself, ". . . had somehow managed to escape. That they thought they could flee from us was pure folly, of course. We had our dogs. We had our torches. They made for quite a spooky effect, the light rippling through the trees, the dogs sniffing and pawing. We fanned out, some of the fellows and myself, to surround them, but after a bit, I seemed to be the only one still on their trail. I have no idea to this day what happened to the others. Again and again, I found and lost them, my two pen-guins, the woods were so knotted, so thick. Finally, I caught them. They were right in front of me, not more than a stone's throw away. They had reached a river and it was impossible to cross."

Poor mamzers, I think.

"I'm about to shout out to them, to order them to stop, to sur-render, when what do we notice right there on the bank? All three of us. We saw it together, at the same time.

"Can you guess it, Herr Jude?

"Not a rock, no.

"Not a cave.

"Exactly. A boat. A small boat, but a boat nonetheless. Someone had tied it to a tree with a rope.

"So, Aha! I think, they've arranged to meet others, have they? Well, we'll see about that!

"Fortunately I hadn't shouted out or in any other way betrayed my presence, for now I could wait to arrest or shoot them all, whatever was necessary."

Whatever was necessary.

"And I crouch down and wait for them, for these others, the ones who have left the boat, to reveal themselves, but they never do. As far as I can tell, there are no others and the boat is there purely by chance. And the two Hasids, Herr Jude, as you call them, what do you imagine they do?

"No, they don't take the boat.

"You or I certainly would take the boat. But not this odd pair. Instead, our little penguins sit upon its edge and debate whether it is permissible, *permissible!*, according to the Laws of Moses, for them to take the boat."

With these words, I am again a boy in cheder, learning the Law on a cold winter's day. All the hairsplitting arguments, such headaches they used to give me!

"One of them is inclined to take the boat," this the head tells me.

"But the other is not so sure. For one thing, they do not have the necessary texts. The one who is inclined to take the boat insists to the other that without the holy books to consult, the only way they can know for certain if they have the right to take the boat is if they *do* take the boat and survive, and then, having survived, consult the books to see if their actions were permissible.

"And if they discover that taking the boat was not permissible, he reasons, because they will have survived, they can at least make reparations to its rightful owner.

"The second one is not so sure. 'What if we take the boat,' he says, 'survive for now, but perish further upriver? Reparations then would be impossible.'

" 'A good point,' the first has to admit, one he had not, in his fear, allowed himself to see.

" 'Plus,' says the second Hasid, 'the boat may very well have holes in it.'

" 'From where do we derive such a supposition?' says the first Hasid.

" 'Why else would someone have abandoned it?'

" 'True,' the first must ruefully admit.

" 'Unless it were useless, it's safe to assume they wouldn't have left it here.'

" 'Aha!' the first one exclaims. 'But if it *is* useless, then it's perfectly permissible to take.'

" 'But why would we take a useless boat?'

"I'm lying in the underbrush," the head tells me, "utterly fascinated and entranced. I'm hanging on every word of this remarkable conversation.

"'Look,' the first one says, 'if the Master of the Universe, Blessed be He, sees fit to place a perfectly good boat in our path in an hour of terrible need, surely it was not that we might perish without consulting the holy books regarding its permissibility!'

"'Could be, could be,' the second Hasid excitedly pulls on his beard.

"'It's an insult to the Law not to take this boat!' the first Hasid says. 'It's an insult to God, God forbid, not to take this boat!'

"What rot! I think to myself, what specious reasoning! They're back exactly where they started! And yet, to my utter amazement, this last argument prevails and the two eagerly help each other into the small boat."

"And did it have holes in it?" I ask reluctantly.

The head laughs and I can feel its laughter on my thigh. "Did it have holes in it? Herr Jude, be sensible! Of course, it had holes in it! Why else would anyone abandon a boat during wartime?"

"And so it sank, then, I suppose."

"It sank, yes," the head chuckles, shaking itself. "Of course, it sank. Only not downward into the river, as you might expect, as I myself expected, but upward, into the sky. The holes, it seems, lightened the craft, so that it was able to leave the river and sail into the night air, which I'm told is rather thick at certain high altitudes."

"And then what happened?" I can't help asking him.

"And then, so engrossed was I in the spectacle before me, two Jews sailing into the Heavens in a boat full of holes, that I didn't see the thick partisan creeping up behind me with his axe and, as everyone knows, he chopped off my head, and that was that."

30

This story sounds vaguely familiar. I wrack my brain, trying to recall where I may have heard it. Then it comes to me. Did I not tell Ola a similar tale concerning two Hasids who sail to the moon and who end up pulling it from the skies? But that was a bedtime story, one which I myself made up!

"Where did you hear this story?" I ask searchingly, pulling the head to me.

Misunderstanding the fervor of my interest, he is pleased to have it nonetheless.

"I saw these things," he insists. "It happened exactly as I have related it." His eyes shine with eagerness, reflecting back my questioning gaze. "But why are you so interested?"

"A coincidence is all," I say, and I drop him on my lap. I'm not about to confide the private details of my personal life to a severed head. "It's only a coincidence."

"It's nearing daybreak, isn't it, Herr Jude?" he says, squinting into the sky.

By degrees, the sky has begun to lighten. Above the tree line and through the braided weave of branches, you can discern a growing halo of blue inside the black, but it's deceptive. If you blink, it disappears.

"Herr Jude," the head repeats, persisting so, that I must fold my arms against my chest. Already, even from our short travels together, I can recognize that tone in his voice, when it loses its edge. He is after something and has left my lap in order to address me more directly.

"What now, little head?" I sigh.

The head clears its throat or at least the upper reaches of it.

"Should I die, Herr Jude," he says, "I mean really die—not this intermediate state of wandering—will you bury me?"

Bury him?

"No," I say, "I can't promise you that."

"I understand," and he looks away.

"The ground is frozen. It will be ages until the spring. I have no tools or shovels."

"Of course."

"It would be unfair of me to promise."

He licks his lips.

"Perhaps you have wondered why I kidnapped you."

I am grateful to him for this change of subjects.

"Ah yes! This preposterous kidnapping!" I say with a false heartiness. A lot of good it has done him. "To tell you the truth, I assumed it was merely something your people did by rote, like calisthenic exercises."

The head grimaces. In the increasing light, I can make out the expression as it distorts his face.

"I have done things, Herr Jude, during the last days of my life, that I never dreamed possible, things which, as a child or even as a young man, I would not have believed myself capable. I don't need to detail them to you. You are only too familiar with the kind of thing I mean. Although I am dead, I fear I haven't much time. After all, how long can I sustain myself without a body? I can't see anything, although I'm used to that. I'm nearsighted, as you know, but this is worse. I've tried to convince myself that it is only a matter of finding my glasses, but I can't lie to myself any longer. My sight is dimming. Is it possible that I am really, finally, going to die? Oh, Herr Jude, it seems like ages since the peasant chopped off my head. My body is lost. We'll never find it, although it was kind of you to humor me. You must believe me when I tell you I kidnapped you for a reason. Not for glory or for country, nor from habit, as you suggest. I assume you are being facetious, although you are right, you are right to chastise me. Only hear me out! I had been watching you for days. For days! It's true. Perhaps because you were less rotted than the others, I was able to persuade myself that I rec-

ognized you from that morning. I needn't explain, I'm sure, which morning I mean. Perhaps it is foolish of me, Herr Jude, to believe that I killed you. But I do. There. It's been said. And is it really so unreasonable an assumption? You look familiar to me. And when I noticed you yesterday, alone, on the edge of your camp, I seized the moment. A ridiculous enterprise, considering my state! And yet, and yet . . ."

"What do you want from me?" I say.

"I need to be forgiven, Herr Jude. Forgive me. Won't you?"

So this is the face of my killer.

"I sicken myself when I think of the things I have done!"

Taking him by the ears, I return him to my lap. He is shivering and perhaps also weeping. It's hard to tell. Apparently, his tear ducts have been severed from the source of their waters in his body, and so if it can be called a weeping, it is a dry weeping. His eyes are cloudy and vague. He is nearly blind and he squints past my face with a tentative, imploring, slightly embarrassed smile on his long and moving lips.

I wrap the scarf tighter around his neck for warmth.

"Little head," I say, "when you killed me, you took everything. My home, my wife, my children. Must you have my forgiveness as well?"

31

There is nothing to do with this head.

The ground is too frozen to bury it properly, and even if it weren't, I have no shovel, no axe, nothing but my bare hands with which to dig a grave. I consider leaving it in the trees and letting the ravens peck at its eyes. And why not? These eyes which aimed this gun at me, the gun which I now hold stupidly in my own hand, why should they not make tasty morsels for the birds? Still, I can't bring myself to do it. The head is dead. What gain could I derive from its desecration? Neither, though, do I wish to be carting it around until spring! The rivers are frozen and even if they weren't, even if they were flowing freely, would letting the fish, instead of the birds, nibble at its eyes and cheeks make any difference?

I walk for I don't know how many versts, carrying the head by its tangled hair with my good hand, the gun strapped across my chest, contemplating this dilemma.

"Look what you've done to me!" I've taken to addressing the head, although thankfully it no longer answers back. "It's bad enough you kill me. Now you leave me with your head!"

God only knows if the poor body is still wandering about, ignorant of its own demise. I half expect to find it crouching behind every other tree. That the head should perish, while I myself persist, is a mystery. However, it was no different for Ola. I have to remind myself of that. Her body lay like a broomstick, inert on her

bed, while her soul flew to the supernal realms. I witnessed it myself. Only we Jews seem destined to haunt this long continent, wandering its lengths, until God, in His wisdom, decrees otherwise.

32

The gun, too, is a problem. I feel absurd toting it about. What a ghastly sight I must make, with my rifle and my severed German head! If I happened upon another Jew or any traveler who could see me, how I would frighten them. I have no idea what makes it shoot or how to determine whether it is loaded, and yet, I feel a very real reluctance to surrender or abandon it. Why leave it to rust in a snowdrift where it will do no one any good? If it succeeds in merely frightening away the wolves, it will have served a purpose. I keep a wary eye out for them each dusk, but either they have not returned or else they have chosen not to reveal themselves. At times, I cannot shake the eerie feeling that I am being watched. A crash will sound in the tall cold grasses and I will turn involuntarily, searching out its source. But they are sly, these wolves, and treacherous. Still, let them come! I'll shake my German's head at them and rattle my gun in their faces, as fierce a sight as they might hope to see!

Perhaps I would have been happier being born a wolf.

A curious thought, but I find I cannot shake it from my head.

Running with a pack, my beard overgrown and shaggy, rutting with a musky mate, we'd produce children who are hard and wild, with cruel and tearing teeth. How they will tear at your throat when you come for them with your specious laws and your cold metal guns.

"Nonsense!" I say aloud. "A fantasy! It's absurd! I am dreaming!" I tell this to the head, whose glazed eyes stare at nothing.

My hand, swollen and infected, aches at the memory of the wolves. The teethmarks, barely discernible now in the puffy flesh, emit an oozing pus. Occasionally, I plunge it up to the wrist in snow, and the biting cold soothes it. I can hardly curl my fingers, and the flesh is turning black.

I will never be a wolf.

I will never be anything other than a dead and mutilated Jew, without even a moon to howl at overhead.

I am lost when the heavy snows begin to fall.

33

I nearly jump, startled by the great *whoosh* of feathers so near to my ear. He flies up, disappearing into the extraordinary whiteness of the sky, and is suddenly before my eyes: a huge black ink spill. Two feathers drop from his plumage into the blood-spattered snow at my feet. I can't take my eyes from this sight, so stirring a picture do the black feathers and the red drops of blood make on the canvas of

white snow. I am lost, mesmerized, in its radiant, shimmering asymmetries.

I have been bleeding again. This, together with my own fatigue, the heavy snowfall, and the burden of the head, has left me paralyzed. Long ago, it seems, I stopped walking, unable to move.

"*Chaimka! Chaimka!*" the Rebbe screams into my ear. I hear him, as if from a distance. My thoughts unravel like a badly knitted garment, until nothing remains but a meaningless tangle. For a moment, I have no idea who I am or what I am doing here. As I stare into the crimson and sable patterns at my feet, they begin to shimmer and move, forming into a face with coal black eyes, ivory skin, and red and dimpled cheeks.

"Ida?" I say. My first wife. She died in childbirth, a girl herself.

"Chaimka," she calls my name, so sweetly, so sweetly, but her distant voice is shrill and piping.

"Ida, I'm cold," I say.

"Chaimka," she says. "You must move! You must move!"

The Rebbe digs his claws into the shoulder of my coat, piercing with them sharply into my skin, forcing me awake. Ida's face is gone. I'm surrounded, I see, by ice-covered trees. The pounding snow is so thick!

"Rebbe, I'm freezing!" I say. "I can't walk! I don't know what to do with this head!"

The Rebbe squawks and caws wildly.

"I don't understand you, Rebbe!" I shout. "Speak in Yiddish, so I can understand!"

From between the spaces in the trees, men appear.

"Careful, careful," each one cautions the others, as though he alone knows what he is doing. They lift and carry me through the woods. Do they have a bier? I cannot tell. My body has lost all feeling. I seem to be lying on my back in their arms. I can see the tops of the trees and the sky moving backwards, behind their shoulders and their heads.

34

Above me an ashen sky of faces, with eyes shining like dark stars. Apparently, I am lying on my back, on a bier of some kind, encircled by a ring of concerned friends and townspeople. Their mouths open and they shower their words down on me, like rain falling from the Heavens.

"Reb Chaim," they shout, as though I were deaf. "You'll soon be all right." "Can you hear us?" "How are you feeling?" "Give him room, give him room, don't crowd him!"

I manage to raise my head a little and see that they have covered me with filthy blankets and have bandaged, as best they can, my infected hand. Beneath the covers, my other hand is empty.

"The head," I whisper.

"Sha, save your strength," one of them says.

A man kneels next to me and murmurs in my ear, "Don't worry, Reb Chaim. We have placed the head in a burlap sack and will carry it with us for you."

After many days, my strength returns and I am able to walk unaided. The men who have carried me, I can tell, are grateful to no longer have me as a burden. I don't blame them. Their kindnesses were more than sufficient. The snow beats down upon us with an unceasing fury. The wind whistles and howls, like a congress of dybbuks. Pushing forward is impossible, but so is standing still.

The world is nothing but snow.

We walk with raised arms, shielding our eyes from its stinging arrows and from its blinding whiteness. The Rebbe sails, not far above our heads, and we strain to hold him in our sights. Even before he was a bird, he was difficult to keep up with.

In the monotony of our travels, we eventually lose count of the days. Except when absolutely necessary, we hardly speak.

Everyone is morose, exhausted, and numb.

35

A small boy named Efraim is the first to see it, during a break in the storm. He is a sickly child, with a leg so badly damaged, it dangles behind him like a puppet, a marionette with broken strings. The littlest student at our yeshiva, he arrived at the pit in the forest that

dark day, with a goose-down pillow under one arm and a tractate of the Talmud tucked beneath the other. This so amused the soldiers they had to cluck their tongues. After shooting first the pillow and then the holy book, they informed Efraim sadly that they had lost their heads. They had misspent his meager allotment of bullets and would now have to beat him to death. And this they did, kicking him swiftly between them, like a small ball in sport. Knocking him in the ribs with their rifle butts, they swept him like so much straw into his grave.

Now affectionately called Pillow by many in our group, he is something of a mascot, our treasure, and every mother's darling.

When, because of his leg, he can walk no further, a great circle of hands will reach down and lift him onto a sturdy pair of shoulders. This honor, however, he accepts only reluctantly and only when he has completely exhausted himself. He prefers to keep up with Reb Elimelech and myself, in our small quorum of elders, hobbling along with a crutch Reb Itzik fashioned for him from a tree.

Now "Reb Chaim! Reb Elimelech!" Efraim shouts from atop a snowy ridge, pointing to the valley on the other side.

"What is it, Pillow?" Reb Elimelech calls out, smiling. The boy likes to play scout.

He calls back, "You must come! Quickly!"

"We must come, we must come," Reb Elimelech shrugs pleasantly to me and I am caught off guard by his warming cordiality. Since our talk that night on the stump, relations between us have been strained

at best. "Do you hear, Reb Chaim?" he says now with a frank and pleasant face. "What does the boy think, we're going to turn and go back?"

"All right, all right, we're coming!" I shout up to him. "Be patient, Pillow."

Together, Reb Elimelech and I climb the snowy hill, stopping on the ridge. Reb Elimelech lays a smooth hand on Pillow's shoulder. The boy leans into him, threading his arms around the shank of Elimelech's thigh. I have tied the burlap sack with the German's head in it around my waist with a rope and the boy will go nowhere near it.

The three of us look down into the valley, startled by what we see.

Below us, not half a verst away, is an old and rambling building, perhaps an estate or a resort of some kind. It's as long as a city block or nearly. Its facade glitters with thousands and thousands of windows, each with its own ornate carving, each catching the light of the sun. A river surrounds it on all sides and its waters appear to be flowing.

"How is this possible?" I say to no one in particular.

"Look at it sparkle," Reb Elimelech hums beneath his breath.

"What is it?" Pillow cries.

"Certainly not water," Reb Elimelech pulls at the silver threads of his beard. "Otherwise it would be frozen."

Behind us, the little town of Jews trudges listlessly through the drifts, too distant for us to hurry them with our calls or excited gestures.

The three of us, Efraim, Reb Elimelech, and myself, look again

towards the sumptuous hotel. I squint for a better look, cupping my eyes with my hands, and see spilling forth from its many door-ways a great tumult of people: bakers in aprons; chefs in tall hats; waiters with starched shirtfronts and shortwaisted coats and long tuxedo tails; a fleet of chambermaids, slimhipped with full bodices beneath their tight pinafores; a line of bellmen, their round hats pushed jauntily to the sides of their heads, each cocked to the left.

Each uniform is a crisp and snowy white.

"A mirage," I say. "We've become snowblind."

"But I see it, too," Reb Elimelech confirms, shielding his eyes with the brim of his hat.

And the people continue to pour forth. Brawny masseuses in loose-fitting clothes, laundresses in knotted babushkas, porters in livery, dishwashers and gardeners, dustmen and groundskeepers. They gather before the main entrance, standing in lines, like a civic group posing for an official photograph. They smile to us, across the distance, waiting for their administrators to join them, which they do and quite soon. The Maître d'Hôtel, the Concierge, and the Hotel's Direktor. Their swift arrivals prompt a smattering of sincere applause from their gathered minions.

"But who are all those people, Reb Chaim?" Pillow asks, hiding now half behind Reb Elimelech, half behind myself.

The Direktor, a heavy man in a bulky blue suit, steps forward, approaching the far side of the river careful not to walk too near

its plashing waters. From there, he raises his hands and beckons to us.

"He's beckoning to you, Reb Chaim."

"To me?" I regard Reb Elimelech dubiously.

"To whom else?" he says.

I scan the Heavens, but there are no helpful birds in sight.

"Herr Skibelski," the stout Direktor calls up the slope with a silver megaphone handed to him, by a bellman, on a silver tray.

"This is Chaim Skibelski," I call back, hanging my cane on the crook of my arm and cupping my hands to my mouth.

"We are ready to receive your party now," the man shouts, again through the silver mouthpiece.

"Eh? What did he say?" Reb Elimelech mutters in my ear.

"He said they're ready to receive us."

Reb Elimelech glances quickly down the slope at the nearly three thousand souls struggling along behind us.

"Dear Heavens," he says, fretting. "I think they've overbooked."

36

We descend the little slope, the three of us, and walk carefully towards the river, the German's head bouncing against my hip. Pillow holds on to the shank of my cane. The slant of the hill is difficult for him with his useless leg.

Nearer, we see that it is not an illusion at all. The river, indeed, is flowing, despite the frosty temperatures. I lift my eyes from its bank and look across at the beardless face of the Direktor, smiling above his tie and the collar of his blue serge suit. His ruddy cheeks glow with health and vigor in this bracing wind, and his blond hair, thinning on top, blows in slightly separating strands.

"Willkommen, willkommen," he says, placing one large hand inside the other. "All is prepared, all is prepared."

Despite the river's churning noises, his voice carries across it. We can hear him easily and he no longer needs the megaphone.

"Excuse me, Herr Direktor, forgive us," I say. "But I don't understand. What exactly have you prepared?"

"Careful, Chaimka," Reb Elimelech mutters through a fist, pretending to stroke his beard.

"Why, your rooms, of course. And all the facilities."

The Direktor turns a good-natured and sardonic face to his staff, all lined up in semicircles behind him. In response, sardonic grimaces appear on each of their faces, as though each had placed a paper mask of the Direktor's likeness over his own.

By this time, our town is catching up with us, straggling forward, sliding down the valley's slope, gathering in a loose congregation at the river's shore. They are nervously quiet, our Jews, uncertain what to make of this cheery group standing in neat lines, all in immaculate white. In the mirror of their robust cleanliness, our own bedraggled and betattered state seems all the more

wretched. But the shame that otherwise might spread through us like a fever is quenched by a natural, if fearful curiosity. After all, who are these people blocking our path? And what do they want from us?

Behind me, I sense a stirring, as those not in the first line bob their heads and stand on their toes to get a better look. Quickly, words are passed from the front to the back of the crowd. *Herr Direktor, Herr Direktor.* Instinctively, I scan the grey, lowering skies. There is not a crow in sight. I glance, quickly, for reassurance, towards Reb Elimelech, but he is staring at the back of his hands. I clear my throat and address the Direktor.

"You say our rooms are ready," I attempt a deferent smile. "However, I do not see a way across this river of yours."

The Direktor smiles broadly, clenching a thick cigar in his sparkling teeth. He pulls at his earlobe and nods towards two burly porters. Stepping forward, they lift him onto their broad shoulders where he sits, between their heads, as though on a small divan.

"Guten Abend," addressing us again through his gleaming megaphone. He is high enough that only those of insufficient height in the far back might have trouble seeing him. "Und willkommen. Welcome to the Hotel Amfortas." He grins congenially. "You are our guests here. Unfortunately, good people, there is no way across the river except through it. A geographical anomaly. Although neither I nor any of my staff have made the trip—we were all born on this side of the shore—I can assure you there is nothing to fear.

Previous visitors to our resort report that the waters are warm and refreshing, restorative, even delightfully so. Please do not be afraid, my dear Jews. You may leave your old clothes on that side of the river. We have fresh things for you here, which I am sure you will find more comfortable than the worn, traveling garments you now possess. So! Who will be the first to cross the river and share in the banquet we are preparing for you here!"

He sweeps a thick arm towards the building behind him. Reflections no longer obscure the views through the hotel's many windows, and we can see waiters inside rolling enormous wheeled carts piled high with tasty-looking foods. They lay shining white tablecloths across long banquet boards. Elegant women arrange vases of bright flowers on each and every table.

"The food is kosher," Herr Direktor notes, "and the flowers we grow in our hothouses."

Although we cannot hear them, a quintet of musicians sways serenely in a corner of the banquet hall. Through the windows of the upper stories, chambermaids are fitting the beds with clean sheets and plump comforters. I imagine them leaving small chocolates or squares of marzipan on every fat pillow, and my mouth begins to water.

"As the day is quickly waning," the Direktor commands in his booming voice, "and there are so many of you, we must begin now or we will never finish by sundown when the river freezes. Please, then," he says, "who will be the first?"

Behind us, the crowd shrinks back, although I confess my reaction is entirely different. I find I'm obsessed with the idea of food. Food! How long has it been since I've eaten? My stomach growls like a bear waking from a winter's nap. At home, with the Serafinskis, this never happened. My sleeping belly was indifferent, completely so, to the parade of food outside its cave. But now, to my growing alarm, I can't seem to concentrate on anything other than the long tables behind the windows, which fill now with the fiery pink reflections of the sky's fading light.

Still, no one moves.

"Juden, please," Herr Direktor calls through the megaphone in order that no one might fail to hear. "Forgive me for being so impatient, so impolite. You are our guests, but the time is drawing short. Who will be the first?"

37

Our motley crowd shrugs, managing to avoid one another's gaze, while prodding each other on with our eyes. A low, murmuring conspiracy envelops us like a dark cloud, casting us in shadow, removing us, if only by degrees, from the questioning eyes of the insistent Direktor and his benevolent staff. I can't help stealing a glance, across the river's waters, at his open, rosy face, so concerned now, his cheeks glowing in the winter wind, the little com-

mas of his nostrils flaring. Our resistance is nothing he hasn't seen before. The sun is failing, the temperatures are dropping, we are all dead. This he knows and uses subtly to his advantage. Why should we sleep another night on the cold, hard ground when there are warm beds, and hot soup is being offered? All we have to do is swim across a river but, still, our fear prevents it.

"I'll do it," a small voice pipes up bravely.

"Pillow?" An astonished Reb Elimelech protectively grabs onto the boy's thin shoulders, holding him back.

"Efraim, don't be ridiculous," I say. "You could easily drown or, worse, freeze."

"Eh? What's this?" the Direktor calls delightedly from across. "Have we a volunteer? Very good, very good!"

"What does it matter, Reb Chaim?" the boy reasons with me. "I'm already dead."

"You think they can't kill us as often as they wish!" I snatch at the boy, pinning him tightly against my legs.

Still, shaking his shoulders, he is able to release himself from my grip. My bitten hand can't hold him. Angry at himself, Reb Elimelech glowers at me, as if to say, *So this is how you abandon a child. Like you abandoned the rest of us!*

"But Reb Elimelech, what am I to do?"

As we stare helplessly at each other, Pillow approaches the river. Its waves have whipped up fearsomely and are churning. Alone, in the snowy field, he looks smaller than ever. Before our cringing

eyes on one side and the subdued urgings of the hotel staff on the other, he removes his flat cap without even a glance back and his frizzy sidelocks sway slightly in the wind.

"That's right," the Direktor calls. "You can throw it on the ground, that's right. You won't be needing it again."

Pillow does as he is told and tosses the cloth headpiece into the snow. He lays down his crutch and unbuttons his coat, pulling it from his thin shoulders and leaving it near his cap. He unbuttons his wool vest and his shirtfront quite gingerly. The purple and scarlet bruises that decorate his narrow chest and his slender back send an anguished current through our crowd. There are gashes where the lime has eaten into him. With a nervous hand, he brushes away a group of maggots that are feeding on his chest.

He might as well be made of paper, he is so thin and frail.

Careful of his leg, Pillow allows his gabardine trousers to fall. Lifting the ruined leg to his chest with both hands, he manipulates it from the compressed cylinder of fabric, then hops once on his good leg, jumping from his fallen pants.

"That's right, boy," the Direktor shouts like a proud father through the silver megaphone. "Show these old fogies what's what, eh!"

From the lines of staff, Pillow receives a polite smattering of applause. It sounds like distant rain. Their encouragement has a chilling effect on the boy's resolve. He looks back, towards me.

But who am I and what do I know? I'm not his father, after all.

What can I tell him? I shrug, my hands opening like a blossom before my chest.

Pillow nods, forgiving me my helplessness. He looks towards the river, dragging his mangled leg behind him, his scrotum tightening in the icy breeze. His back twists as he rows with his shoulders and elbows, compensating for the leg.

The staff stomps and cheers his every step and the Direktor claps his hands smartly, bringing forth, from the bathhouse, two big peasant women. Their hair is braided in tight loops against their heads and each carries a thick woolen towel, as long as a shroud. They kneel, on one knee, by the far shore, ready to greet the boy who trembles on the other side, from fear or cold I cannot tell. His efforts and all the attention have exhausted him. Before him, the river boils and rages, as if stirred by a giant spoon.

"Ready when you are, Pillow," the Direktor trumpets, having learned the nickname from our nervous calls. "Jump as far upriver as you can because the current will pull you down."

Obligingly, Pillow limps two or three meters upriver, and before anyone can say anything, the moment has passed. The boy has jumped in.

"That's it, that's it!" the Direktor calls.

"Help! Help me!" Pillow cries out, flailing, his small head bobbing up and disappearing beneath the river's flashing surfaces. With only one leg, how did we expect him to swim!

Laughing, the Direktor fishes him to the other side with his long

and sturdy pole. Pillow latches onto its hook, sputtering and coughing, and the Direktor reels him in, lifting his slight body easily out of the waters. The river washes from his blushing torso, his teeth clatter, and the peasant women swath him in their towels. Hugging him between them, they smother him in their expansive bosoms, drying him with the long strokes of their bare and muscular arms.

"They're squeezing the life out of him!" a woman behind me screams in protest, but when the two women release him from their cloth prison, the boy jumps up on two sturdy legs, waving happily across the river's rush.

The two peasant women smile, dimples in their apple cheeks.

Gone are the bruises and the scars, the deep red gashes where the rifle butts tore his flesh. Pillow is whole again, his body healed. He stands, naked, his arms raised in triumph above his shining head. His thin belly is curved slightly, bending back, and his hairless penis hangs to the side.

"Pillow, tell your friends what the river is like," Herr Direktor urges, while the one attendant wraps the boy in a thick white bathrobe, and the other places thongs upon his feet.

"The water is warm and alive!" Pillow calls in a happy girlish voice. "Almost toasty!"

"Warm and toasty," calls the Direktor. "Did you hear that, Jews?"

The staff roars its approval, and it isn't long before the whole of us are shedding our worn, worm-eaten, bullet-pocked clothing,

and moving in a naked, talkative throng towards the river's lip. The snow freezes our bare feet and we hop and skip and jump in, splashing like children on a hot summer day.

The river is warm and alive, indeed, with a quality nearer to light than to water. It whirs and hums electrically, buzzing against our ears, clothing our nakedness in shimmering cocoons. Its spangling incandescence fills every hole in my body. I open my mouth, below the surface, and let the golden, lambent, flashing phosphorescence fill it.

I can't help laughing, so painfully ticklish is the experience. Kicking with my legs, I force myself down, away from the dull sky, and towards the river's bottom, curious about its substance. It seems to be of ordinary mud and I let the handful I've lifted float between my fingers.

The burlap bag with the German's head falls to pieces in these stinging, electric waters. The head sinks to the bottom of the river floor, its eyes closed, its hair floating upward. Before I can grab it, a jolt of searing pain courses through my chest, knocking me back and away. My lungs have expanded within me! I struggle not to breathe the river in and swim blindly towards the surface. A flurry of hanging legs blocks my way. They dangle in the water like thick river weeds. I can't get through and am drowning!

Hands break the silvery surface, but I am too slippery. Like a fish, I slip continually from their grasp. More hands grapple for me, bracing

me, hauling me up. My head, finally, cleaves through the light and a thick knot of peasant women drops me, naked and dripping, onto the shore.

I cough and sputter, vomiting up lines of liquid light, the salty air caustic in my nose.

Smirking through his plump and golden-ruddy face, the Direktor kneels in the snow and slaps me on the back.

"Too much of a good thing, old man?" He laughs. "Eh? Too much of a good thing!"

The peasant women swaddle me roughly in their towels, rubbing them across my face.

"Careful of my wounds!" I shout, but I can tell by the way their towels caress my face that they are gone. I hold up my hand and see that the wolf bite has healed.

38

My suite is spacious, with warm cream walls above a coffee-brown wainscoting. Bouquets fill the rooms. Lilies, white roses, an explosion of chrysanthemums. From the hotel's greenhouse, or so the attached note says. A woven basket in the shape of a whale holds fruits and chocolates, wheels of cheese, and a bottle of plum brandy in its mouth, all tied with ribbons and fancy strings. There are two shot

glasses, next to the brandy, and I wonder if I will be sharing the suite with someone else. Perhaps Reb Elimelech. If so, there is much, I'm afraid, that needs saying between us.

In the spirit of experimentation, what will it hurt if I take a taste, I remove a red pear from the wicker whale and shine it on my sleeve. Reciting the blessings for the first fruits, I take a bite, not too large, in case I have to spit it out. Since my death, food has been like wood pulp in my mouth. Hard, tasteless, dry. Impossible to swallow, it blocks your throat, until you must painfully cough it up.

And so the bite of pear I take is small and of a manageable size. I allow my teeth to caress the outer skin, ripping the barest hemisphere of meat. This I lay, provisionally inert, upon my flat tongue. Slowly, the juices leave the small coin and drop bitingly across my tongue, filling my mouth with its searing delights. Unable to keep still, the tongue lifts itself, pressing the fruit against the roof of my mouth, and I am stunned by the sweetness flowing into my throat, where the taste now explodes. Impossible to restrain, my unprepared tongue shifts the fruit between my teeth, which pulverize it into gritty paste, extracting every ounce of its flavor. The tongue rolls in this paste, like a delirious bridegroom in his wedding bed.

But my mouth can take no more and my gullet lurches forward, greedily pulling at the pap, and causing a drop to spill onto my chin.

I nearly have to sit down, and grab hold of the table for support. Tears flow from my eyes. I wipe them on my sleeve, unable to catch my breath.

"Well," I say to myself. "Oh, but the things we forget!"

Another bite and I am dancing about the room, but that is all that I can take. I lay the nibbled pear onto a silver pear-shaped tray, which seems to have appeared from nowhere. It's just as well. There is a knock at the door. With a napkin I daub the juices from the corners of my lips and my beard, and quickly dry my fingertips.

As I walk towards the door, my tongue flicks through my teeth, searching out the threads of pulp that have lodged in the spaces between them. Adjusting my robe, girding its belt around my girth, I run a quick hand through my hair and clear my throat.

"Yes?" I say, leaning against the door.

"Herr Skibelski?"

"Yes?"

"*Chaim* Skibelski?"

"Yes, I am Chaim Skibelski."

"We have your suit, sir."

"My suit?"

"Yes, sir."

I open the door a crack. The small bellman is dressed in a stiff white uniform with two rows of golden buttons running, in parallel lines, up and down his chest. He holds a woolen suit before him on a wooden hanger.

"I don't understand," I say.

"For dinner, sir. For this evening. You'll find socks and undergarments, everything else you need, in your wardrobe and the chest of drawers."

"In my wardrobe and drawers?"

"In your suite, sir."

I must stare at him in complete incomprehension, until he raises the hanger even higher, indicating that I should take the suit, which I eventually do.

"Thank you, sir," he says.

I'm completely bewildered.

"If there's anything else you need . . ."

"No, no," I say, patting the empty pockets of my robe, searching for a gratuity.

He clicks his heels, bowing from his chest.

"Very well, then. Thank you, sir."

And he pushes his wheeled cart, with its evening suits and its formal dresses, to the door across, where he also knocks. Glancing over his shoulder, he nods at me quickly. A small, polite gesture of dismissal.

"Herr Lipinski," he says.

"Yes?" comes the nervous voice.

"*Nahman* Lipinski?"

"Yes, I am Nahman Lipinski."

"Sir, we have your suit."

I shut my door and lean against it, holding the suit at arm's length, the better to inspect it. Nothing should amaze me anymore, and yet I am quite unprepared to see that not only does the coat seem the perfect size, but it looks exquisitely tailored. Indeed, I

peel back the front lapel and read: *Custom tailored for Chaim Skibelski by Schwartz & Schneider, Fine Tailors of Germany*. I remove my robe, tossing it across the large bed in the next room, and have barely managed to slip into the pants and jacket, when someone else is at the door. I make my way through the suite, my grizzled chest bare beneath the coat.

"Yes?" I say, speaking again through the wood.

"Herr Skibelski?"

"I am Chaim Skibelski," I say, opening the door.

"With the compliments of the staff, sir."

Another bellman, in an identical uniform, stands against the white wall and offers me an open humidor filled with large, oily cigars.

"These are for me?" I say.

"With the compliments of the staff."

"Danke," I say.

"Bitte sehr," he nods, acknowledging my use of his language. "You'll find matches in your coat pocket, I believe."

"Thank you again," I say, a cigar between my teeth.

"Dinner is in the main ballroom. And you'll be taking the steam afterwards?"

"The steam?"

He consults a list pinned to a board with a large metal clip.

"My mistake, sir. Your name is not on for the steam tonight."

"No matter," I say, brightly. "It's just as well."

"A pleasant evening then."

"And for yourself."

He steps back, clicking his heels, and disappears into the white corridor. I clutch the humidor to my chest, lost not in thought but completely outside of it, my head as empty as the Holy Ark on Simchas Torah.

I place the humidor upon the table, near the wicker whale. Engraved on the brass plate around its keyhole are my initials, *C.S.* Well, why should it surprise me to find my old humidor in this hotel, after all the many years it sat, like a faithful djinn, upon my desk?

I reopen the box, it's unlocked, and its various perfumes rise about me in pungent clouds. I inhale deeply, astonished that I can. What a magnificent place the Rebbe has brought us to! The suite fills with the tobacco's marvelous, acrid scents, bringing with them a host of memories. My days in the forest, inspecting lumber and buying acres of trees, are returned to me, like a parcel lost at a railway station. *Excuse me, sir, but I believe you dropped this.* Where was I going that day when I dropped my package on the railway platform? Oh yes, to Warsaw for a grandson's bris. Was it Solek's or Izzie's or perhaps even Kubuś'?

Lowering two fingers into the jacket pocket, I bring them together and raise the box of matches concealed there by some conscientious tailor. *Thank you, Messrs. Schwartz & Schneider.* A scratch against the side, a sulphurous spark, I bite the nib and the cigar is

alight and in my mouth. I draw the flame of the match up through the cylinder, puffing, and turn it to inspect its fragrant tip. Its leaves are as red as a hot coil. I inhale shallowly, the wet end against my tongue. My neck relaxes, the tension disappears from behind my eyes. I could easily sit here on the bedside all night, but soon it will be evening, and I must hurry to dress.

So, with the cigar in my mouth, I remove the coat and pull on the shirt they have provided, fastening the square cuff links into the starched white sleeves. I put my arms into the wool vest, threading my gold chain, with its fobs, through its little holes. I tuck my watch into a pocket. Nearly four o'clock. It's already dark outside.

I stand before the mirror and tie the tie, my hands working nimbly beneath my chin, my cigar jutting into the air, so that I resemble a clarinetist in a klezmer orchestra. I put on the jacket, adjusting its sleeves, and flick a bead of lint from its lapel. I brush my hair and remove the cigar from my mouth to comb my beard. I spit a scrap of tobacco from my mouth, positioning it on the tip of my tongue with my teeth.

A splash of cologne, a diamond stick pin for my tie, one more puff, and with my cigar between my fingers and my cane against my palm, I brace myself for a look into the mirror.

My face is, once again, itself, my eye no longer a milky opal. A small smile caresses my lips. But is it me? Or a photograph from my

late middle age? So hale and hardy do I seem, dashing even, in these wondrous clothes.

"Chaim Skibelski," I lean towards the silvered glass. "Where in the name of God have you been?"

39

I have often thought how pleasant it would be to live in a hotel, to live as a guest, and have everything provided you. Your furnishings, your meals, all of life's dreary chores seen to by a large and helpful staff, many of whom are experts in their fields. If you want tea, you press a button and a boiling samovar arrives. After a long day of work, perhaps you feel the need to relax. And so, with a discreet word in the concierge's ear, a horse is saddled and, within the hour, you are flying across the grounds in the whorling light of dusk, not a care in the world. Your stomach is empty, but so what? You may eat in the restaurant or have the meal sent up to your rooms. There is no hurry, no schedule to keep. You may change into your clothes leisurely, taking time, if you wish, for a massage, before meeting a friend or two in the bar while your table is prepared.

Outside my window, the sun lowers itself into the forests. Dark silhouettes move against the pattern of the trees. The figures call out to one another, carrying long poles.

I close the light in my room. The hallway outside my suite is

bright and humming with activity. Porters scurry about, white-capped chambermaids and pageboys rush quickly by, offering the briefest of nods, inquiring with only a look whether you are in need of anything.

A white carpet covers the stone floors, muffling my steps and the tap of my cane. I pass familiar men and women dressed elegantly for dinner with their children. We greet each other with appreciative nods and tart, concealed smiles. To look at us now, who would imagine that only this afternoon we were wandering through the snows, worm-eaten and morose? The corridors are hung with intricate tapestries, depictions of hunting parties and scenes of courtly love. Glittering mirrors cover the walls between them. These we pass, looking secretly into our own bedazzled eyes.

Is it possible that we actually belong here?

"Going down!" the liftboy sings and we squeeze into the lift, a thick gaggle of us, drawing ourselves in tightly so as not to crease each other's clothes.

In the foyer, a rush of languages flies about our ears. The Direktor can be heard barking orders in German, the Maître d'Hôtel welcoming new arrivals in French. At a telephone station behind the reception desk, the head chef, a tall man in a white stove-pipe hat, screams in Italian, perhaps to a negligent wholesaler. The waiters address each other in either Rumanian or Greek.

In the alcoves of the bar, beneath the arches and the great porticos, and all along the staircases with their winding iron rails, guests

converse in English, in Spanish, in Czech, and, God knows, in seventy other languages.

A child falls and cries for its mother in Serbo-Croatian and is picked up and comforted by a stranger speaking Dutch with a Turkish accent!

In the bar, men in evening jackets press their heads together. One finishes speaking and the others lean back, roaring in laughter. A woman in furs puffs on a slender brown cigarette. She nods at her companion, who replies with a mouthful of smoke.

Murals cover every wall, cloudlike horses leaping over curly fields of heather, their riders pursuing a dancing fox.

I close my eyes and listen to the pleasing din of bottles ringing, jewelry clinking, cash registers clanging, coins falling like raindrops onto silver trays.

"Nu, Chaimka?" a warm voice whispers into my ear. I open my eyes.

Reb Elimelech stands before me, in a white caftan. His long beard, newly trimmed, spills like milk across his narrow chest. We kiss each other and sit on stools, our backs against the bar.

"Not bad, eh?" he says, and what a joy it is to add the small spice of our Yiddish to this simmering stew of sounds.

A dark-faced waiter inquires after our drinks. We settle on kvass, which he ferries from another bar at the far end of the room. We watch him, winding through the crowd, balancing the tall glasses on a tray held, with one hand, high above his head.

"L'chaim," we toast, and the first sip goes down quite smoothly to the bottoms of our empty stomachs.

"I'd forgotten all about this," Reb Elimelech says, stunned in a moment of serene joy. "Drinking!" he says. "An amazing thing!"

A quintet of musicians serenades us from a corner of the room.

Reb Elimelech passes his lucent eyes over the glowing wall lanterns and the hanging chandeliers, across the murals and the smooth-faced barmen standing beneath them in starched jackets and purple-black bow ties, their hair combed back and gleaming with pomade.

"Chaim," he says, pausing long enough for me to look him in the face. "Forgive me."

The musicians finish to indifferent applause.

"No, if only I had thought to help you," I begin to stammer, reaching for his knee, but suddenly, the Maître d'Hôtel is before us, pressing his hands together as though he were rolling a knish.

"Pardon, pardon, messieurs," he says. He wears a grey flannel cutaway with swallowtails and a foulard folded perfectly, like a royal blue rose, in its breast pocket. On his other chest blooms a dainty boutonniere. A miniature chandelier and our faces, slightly con-vexed, are reflected in his twinkling monocle. "Allow me to escort you to your tables."

With a final pull of kvass, we set our glasses on the bar and fol-low the little fellow into a brightly lit hallway. Out of sheer joy, Reb Elimelech links his arm into mine, patting my hand, and we walk

together down the long corridors, like kings, smiling into each other's beaming face, fully reconciled.

Stopping briefly, and only once, to peruse his reservation book, the Maître d'Hôtel leads us into a banquet hall the size of an ocean liner. White linens float before us, like broken cakes of ice in an Arctic sea spreading endlessly to the horizon. It's an illusion. Ceiling-high mirrors in the many tall archways stretch the room to infinity. Even without the mirrored replication, the hall must actually be quite large, although it's impossible to tell. Already Jews from our town are seated at many of the tables, sneaking bits of bread and butter while waiting for the rest of us to arrive and be guided to our seats.

"This way, this way," the Maître d'Hôtel says to Reb Elimelech. "Wait here, Monsieur Skibelski, and I will return for you in a nonce."

"But why can't we sit together?" I say, feeling suddenly abandoned. "We are old friends."

"Alors, monsieur," he says, burnishing with a raised knuckle the twin wings of his mustache. "I have thousands of people to seat. Your Rebbe has established the order. We must follow it to the letter, I'm afraid. Understand. For nothing has been left to chance."

It is my first meal in I don't know how many years. How good and pleasant it would be to share it with a friend. But the Maître d' insists, and I must watch as Reb Elimelech is led away to a table in the middle distance. There, he is welcomed with handshakes and light kisses. They make a space for him, adjusting their chairs. A carafe of water is passed to him, which his nearest neighbor intercepts, pour-

ing until Reb Elimelech's glass is full. He lifts the goblet to his lips with his long tapered fingers, staining his mustache a slightly deeper white.

"Monsieur Skibelski, if you will."

I follow the strutting Maître d' through the crowd, greeted variously on all sides. The tables are filling up. How splendid and fashionable we all look, even the town's poor and its beggars. With bright eyes and rosy cheeks, we have the faces of the newly born.

The Maître d'Hôtel approaches a large round table with an empty chair. This, he pulls out for me. Wistfully, I search the room one last time for Reb Elimelech. There he is, laughing and joking, cracking his knuckles at his table of friends. Perhaps there is some mistake. Why must I be seated with a group of strangers, although they seem pleasant enough, while everyone else is matched with dear comrades and old friends?

"Monsieur, your seat."

The place card, indeed, reads *Chaim Skibelski*.

Resigned, I lower myself into the chair and greet the table with a dignified nod.

"Good evening," I say, too unhappy and shy to look at more than their hands. "I am Chaim Skibelski. It's a pleasure to make your acquaintance at this lovely hotel."

My words tumble, like inexperienced mountain climbers, into a silent abyss. Looks are traded all around the table. There are grins and frowns and kneaded brows. There is something comical, obvi-

ously, about my presence here, a stranger left to fend for himself in the midst of this tightly knit family.

Finally, one of the women clears her throat and addresses me, sternly.

"Papa," she says, "don't you even know us?"

40

Instinctively, I pat my pockets in search of the photographs I took from our house, but they, of course, are in my other suit, which I abandoned in the snow. I scan the faces at the table, comparing them to my memories of these photos. But why should it be that I can recall their pictures more clearly than my children's actual faces?

In any case, here they are before me, my daughters: Sarah, Edzia, Miriam, Hadassah. I silently sound their names. How beautiful, how beautiful they are. Sarah, with her dark eyes and her arms folded below her bosom. Her sister Edzia has grown stout. I've never seen her so matronly. She waits for me to speak. Mirki suppresses a bold laugh. It is caught, trembling, in her throat. She has her mother's triangular eyes and her face flashes with delight. What a nice joke they've played on me, she is thinking. My littlest one, Hadassah, looks so sad and worried, with her curving nose and her troubled brow.

Their brother Lepke picks at a kaiser roll. A thin, nervous boy, he tears it to bits, without eating so much as a scrap.

My sons-in-law are here as well. Sarah's Markus, bald and round as the number eight. Edzia's scrappy Pavel, a little rooster of a man. Mirki's skinny Marek, as scrupulously elegant as a concert pianist. And Hadassah's Naftali Berliner, new to the family. They were married less than a year before the war, these two. Now he solicitously holds her small hand, as her searching eyes never leave mine.

I address the table, looking at my useless hands.

"You are telling me that not one of you survived?"

I cringe to hear my words. I did not intend to sound such a harsh rebuke.

"We are sorry, Papa," says Sarah, and the others murmur in concurrence.

"And your children?" I say, roaring like a lion, despite myself. "Where are my grandchildren?"

At nearby tables, people turn away, trying not to look at us.

"Sshh, Papa, they're right here."

"Papa, quiet down!"

The children's table is next to ours. Solek and Izzie, Pola, Kubuś, and Sabina sit with Mirki's twin daughters whose names I can't remember.

They shyly call "Hello, Zeyde" to me, the boys in miniature

suits and uncomfortable ties, the girls in wintery frocks, but it's a solemn greeting, as though they had recently been scolded by their parents on my behalf and are now uncertain how I will treat them.

"Forgive us, Papa," Hadassah repeats, and her new Naftali tightens his grip on her little hand, signaling her to let him speak on their behalf.

"Papa Chaim," he says. "There was nothing we could do. They wouldn't let us run or even bribe them to escape."

"It's nothing, it's nothing," I say, raising my fingers in protest. "Let us never mention it again."

"I came looking for you, Papa," this from Mirki.

"I know. I know, I heard."

"In Suwalk, Papa, but there was no one left."

"You were lucky you got back," her Marek says.

"And Shmuel and Regina?" I ask.

"In a Russian labor camp," says Sarah.

"Thank God," says Edzia.

"Thank God," I say.

"Behind the Urals," adds Mirki.

"And they're alive?"

"They're alive, they're alive."

"They arrested us together," my Lepke volunteers.

"For illegally crossing the border, Papa Chaim."

"We had to," says Lepke.

"Of course. They had to."

"Of course," I say.

"There was no escaping otherwise."

Everyone is talking at once.

"Two weeks we were together, Shmuel, Regina, and I," Lepke says, tearing his bread into smaller and smaller pieces.

"In a prison in Minsk, they were."

"But after that, I didn't see them."

"And your mother?" I say, looking at them around the table.

"She's upstairs," they tell me.

"Dressing."

"She's dressing."

4 1

We look sadly at one another across the doorframe, not needing to speak, understanding everything at once. Her face is more familiar to me than my own. I watched it grow old, every night, every morning, for most of my life, all but the first twenty years or so. Even now, after looking into it for only half an instant, I must remind myself to *see* it, to see it fully, and not allow myself to grow so accustomed to its presence that it all but disappears.

"Chaimka," she says, privately, in a small and nervous gasp.

She is a large, blunt woman, strong and stubborn as an ox. I take hold of her thick arm and she pulls me into her suite.

"Ester," I say.

In a thin shift, she throws her body, as thick as a small tree, into mine. Nearly crushing me in her grip, she kisses my neck and my face. Her breath is soft and warm and slightly malodorous.

I close the curtains and pour two glasses of brandy. Her suite also has a whale, also filled with food and drink.

"Ester," I say. "My God! Ester! Let us sit and have a drink!"

"A drink? Chaimka! You'll ruin your dinner."

"One drink is not going to ruin anything. Just to celebrate, Ester! Why don't you sit, like I'm telling you."

I button the dress she has chosen in back for her and she finally sits primly, although slightly annoyed, her large body on the edge of a stuffed loveseat. She removes the pins from her hat and lays the hat across her bare shins. She accepts the glass, but does not drink from it. I smile at her and throw the liquid back to the very ends of my throat, where it burns pleasantly. I never learned to sip a drink. I pour a second shot and loosen my tie. Holding the bottle in one hand, the small glass in the other, I sit near her, on the loveseat.

"Well," I say seductively.

"Chaim," she says darkly, a tone of warning in her voice.

And before I know it, we are crying in each other's arms. I'm on my knees before her, my heaving belly in her lap.

42

"Come on, Chaimka," she says, whispering in my ear. "You're not a baby now."

She beats my back with her hard fat hand. I look into her face. She has already wiped away her tears. There are wet smudges on her cheeks. "Are we little children, that we should cry?"

This she says and I nod. She is right, of course. We are not children. But a man can still mourn. Or must he be a child for that?

Ester sips her drink and removes her shoes. She stretches out her feet. Lifting first one foot and then the next into her hands, she rubs her toes.

"Such shoes they give me!"

"You'd be more comfortable in your old shoes," I say, sitting up.

AT THE TABLE, Pavel is demonstrating some point with his hands, moving them closer and closer together with each phrase.

"A town shrinks into a ghetto. A ghetto into a train car. A train car shrinks into . . ."

But they are too difficult for me to hear, these accounts of their deaths. They are my children, after all, and I feel the need to mourn them, to rip my clothes, to sink to the floor in my grief. But how can I, when they are all sitting before me, eating and laughing, jostling each other with their elbows?

"That's nothing," says Markus, and he describes how they drowned him, holding his head in a bucket of freezing water.

"But why?"

"A medical experiment," he says, and he cannot stop laughing. "Doctors from Berlin to Frankfurt are probably drowning their patients at this very moment, all thanks to me!"

He puffs merrily at his cigar.

"Markus, please," Sarah scolds him. "People are trying to eat."

He was always something of a happy vulgarian, although quite good in business.

"That's right, that's right," he guffaws. "Don't let a little thing like my death spoil your dinner." And they all laugh with him, but the talk disturbs me.

How is it possible for men to make laws against another man's life, so that by merely living, he is guilty of a crime? And what kind of men enforce such laws, when they could be out on a clear day, boating or hiking or running to their mistresses instead?

"Chaimka," my Ester says quietly.

She can read my thoughts, so familiar is she with the patterns they create as they cross my face. And that is all she needs to say, *Chaimka*, meaning *It's not up to one murdered Jew to solve the problems of the world!*

Meeting her eyes, I look again into their familiar triangular shapes. She is uncomfortable in her stiff new clothing. She is bored, with nothing to do. Her large hands tap a fork against the table top. She does not like waiting to be served, but would rather be herself serving, running from the kitchen to the table, with bowls and ladles and bread and knives and dishes for everybody else.

She sighs, heaving her heavy chest, and I fear that I did not love her sufficiently, that I did not give to her the affection that was her portion, as another, more cheerful husband might have done. I was too preoccupied with my accounts and my ledgers, with my shipments of lumber and my forests to buy, with sending this child to America before that army could snatch him away or buying that child from this army when he couldn't be sent in time.

When I married her, also, I was still grieving over Ida, my first wife. She had died some months before, so small and frail and unable to bring a baby into the world.

"Chaimka!" my Ester repeats.

"Ester," I say. "I can't help it. Let me sit here and think. What harm does it do?"

43

The soup arrives in a lion-legged tureen. The waiter, in a sharp white cutaway, places it smoothly in the center of the table. He twirls the black wings of his mustache, which the soup's steam has dampened, and ladles out a bowl for each of us, the women first and then the men. He never spills a drop as he orbits our table with bowl after bowl, until we are all sitting behind rising veils of steam.

The soup is delicious and warm.

"Mama," says our Hadassah, "it tastes just like your soup."

Ester blows on her first spoonful and lifts it to her mouth. She keeps the broth on her tongue for a moment, tasting it completely.

Then, "No, no, sheyne," she says, swallowing. "I never used such basil. This is how your bubbe made it."

"I was thinking the same thing," says Naftali Berliner. "I was thinking that this was *my* mother's soup."

In fact, I myself had the same impression, that the recipe was my mother's.

"Let me taste," Hadassah says to her Naftali, and soon bowls are being exchanged around the table. The dead, we tell ourselves, needn't worry over germs.

And the results of our investigations? No matter what bowl we drink from, everyone's soup tastes like his mother's. Only my daughters' and son's soup taste the same.

"But they came out of the same pot!" Marek exclaims.

"I watched the waiter dish it out himself!" from Pavel. He wipes his spoon in his napkin and brings it to the edge of the tureen.

"May I?" he says, asking our permission.

"By all means," we consent. "Go ahead." And "Please."

He skims his spoon into the broth and raises its contents to his lips. He blows on it and takes a taste, snapping his tongue against the roof of his mouth.

"It's my mother's soup," he says. "I'd know it anywhere," tears welling in his eyes.

"But it's not your mother's at all," says Edzia, tipping a spoonful onto her flat tongue. "It isn't burnt, for one thing."

"It's true," Pavel says to the rest of us. "My mother always burnt her soup. But this soup is burnt as well," and he points at the tureen, shaking his finger for emphasis.

We repeat the experiment, each dipping our spoon directly into the tureen. Our initial impressions are confirmed. We are each eating our own mother's soup.

I see her bending over her large pot, my mother. "Go wash," she scolds. Her face is tense. She's getting a migraine. "Go wash before the soup gets cold!"

I had always secretly hoped to see her again. One more of the afterlife's bitter disappointments. Her people were not strong and business-minded like the Skibelskis, but frail and hopeless. And such dreamers! Of her siblings, she was the only one to marry. The others, my aunts and my uncles, busied themselves with storytelling and other useless occupations. Our Lepke takes after this side of the family, unfortunately. In the end, the rough world of family life and trade proved too much for my mother, and she died when I was young, before I had made anything of myself, before I could say to her the things a son wants to and must.

I look up to see that even Markus is crying.

"Pardon me," I say to the waiter as he ladles another bowl for everyone.

"Yes, Herr Skibelski?"

He pauses in his work, holding the dripping ladle above a starched white cloth.

"This soup," I say.

"It was to your satisfaction, I hope?"

"Exquisite, yes, excellent," I say. "I was just wondering."

"Sir?"

"What do you call it?"

He places one arm on his hip and twirls the ladle flirtatiously.

"For you, Herr Skibelski," he says, "I'd call it Keila's soup."

He smiles like a man caught at some pleasurable taboo.

"Keila's soup?" I say.

"Yes, sir."

"After my mother?"

He winks, lifting the tureen from the table.

"Quite a recipe, isn't it?"

44

My sons-in-law's names appear on the list for the steam and they are each given a small blue card with their appointment time handwritten upon it. Although he is not interested, my son Lepke also is given an appointment. Only my name is absent from the list.

"There will be other opportunities," the Maître d'Hôtel mews, scanning the names on his sheets. "Shortly, my colleague Frau Gruber will be here to assist with the women," and he bustles over to the nearest table.

"It's quite relaxing, they say," says Marek, tapping his card with his long index finger.

"By the looks of it, they'll be running all night," this from Markus.

"What time are your appointments? Perhaps we can meet and go together," Pavel peers at his own card and then at the others through small round eyeglasses.

"Not until the middle of the night."

"Amazing," Pavel removes his glasses. "The staff must never sleep."

"Three in the morning?" Markus grunts, looking over Lepke's appointment card, a cigarette hanging from his lip. The boy holds on to the card awkwardly, as though embarrassed to have hands. "They'll send someone to call for you. You needn't worry. They'll make sure that you're awake."

When alive, Markus traveled a great deal for his work and so is familiar with hotels and their ways.

"Once in Vienna," he tells the table, "I met a remarkable man over dinner, a Herr Goldstein, a real talker, and the two of us stayed up nearly till dawn, the entire time talking in the lobby. There we were, in two stuffed chairs, while the night staff cleaned all about us!"

45

After the sumptuous dinner and many long speeches, both from the hotel administration and from the heads of our local councils and other civic groups, cigars are distributed and the men are free to smoke.

"I've made discreet inquiries," Marek leans in closer to the table, lowering his voice.

"And what have you found?" Pavel murmurs.

"Nothing conclusive, I'm afraid."

"You've tried bribes?" Markus bellows, despite himself. His voice is always booming. It's impossible for him to speak softly. Even his whisper is too loud.

"Inquiries into what?" I say. I'm a little drunk, I fear, and still in a stupor from the food.

"Bribes? Of course, I haven't tried bribes."

"Why not?"

"We haven't any money."

Markus snorts. "What's money have to do with it?"

"To do with what?" I say. "What are you talking about?"

"Lepke," says Pavel. "Explain it to your father."

But Lepke only looks at his chest, his cheeks reddening.

"Leave the boy alone," says Marek.

If I can't understand them, what hope is there for Lepke?

"What are you suggesting?" says Pavel to Markus. "That we bribe them with the very items they've supplied for us?"

"Among other things," says Markus, removing his cigar and rolling his tongue inside his mouth.

"I've talked to everyone I can. From the Assistant to the Direktor to the chambermaids."

"Oh, the chambermaids! Now we understand."

Marek bristles, sweeping his hair back with a long pale hand. "Markus, not everyone lives in the gutter like you."

"Not everyone is so lucky," burps Markus.

"But are they hiding something," says Pavel, "or do they simply not know anything?"

"About what?" I say. "Know what?"

"Chaim," sighs Pavel, "forgive us—"

Marek interrupts him. "It's just that some of us aren't content like you to follow a grackle halfway across Europe without even so much as asking where we're going!"

"A grackle?" I say. The word is unfamiliar to me.

"Jackdaw, grackle, whatever."

"But the Rebbe isn't a grackle," I say. "He's a crow."

"Exactly my point!"

"Marek," warns Markus.

"Papa Chaim," says Pavel, "he doesn't mean any disrespect."

But Marek snorts disdainfully and crosses his long arms against his slender chest. "Don't I?"

They are modern young men, these three. Zionists, Bundists, freethinkers for all I know.

"If it were up to him," sneers Marek, "we'd all be traipsing after crows."

Marek, I'm told, was even once a member of the Communist Party, although Miriam refused to confirm or deny this when I confronted her.

"Marek, leave it alone," Hadassah calls from their side of the table, listening in and standing up for her father. She's not afraid of an elder brother-in-law. At times, I worried she was much too attached to me and that was what kept her from marrying.

"He may be a crow, Marek," I say, "but at least he survived!"

"So he survived? So what?"

"Did being a man help you when it came to that?"

"Marek, Chaim," says Pavel. "All we want to know is where we are and what will happen to us here."

"Then you'll have to bribe people to find out," bellows the rotund Markus.

"Markus, for God's sake, keep your voice down!" Marek hisses. "People are listening!"

"But isn't it clear?" Lepke pipes up in his weak and quavering voice. We can barely hear him.

"What's clear?" his brothers-in-law ask, smirking with their heads together, like conspirators.

So shy, he cannot look them in the face, Lepke pinches at his chin, taps his thumb against his teeth and then dries his wet nail across his lower lip.

"That we're in the World to Come," he says. "Isn't it clear?"

46

It's strange. He's a sweet boy, our Lepke, but if you didn't pay close attention, you might forget that he is here. Because his mind is vague and he isn't a sharp businessman like the others, no one credits what he says. Also, he cannot meet their gazes or stand against their thundering retorts. He's too polite to contradict them. And so, instead, he folds up into himself and disappears.

"Spare me your fairy tales!" cries Marek.

"What's so fantastic about it?" says Lepke.

"All this nonsense they cooked up to enslave us, these rabbis!"

"But is it so far-fetched," says Pavel, "given our situation."

"Look," booms Markus. "If there is a Paradise, do you actually think they'd let Jews into it?"

47

My sons-in-law blather on, lost in the thickening cloud of their cigar smoke. It floats about their heads in grey and fuzzy plumes.

I sit back and freshen my mouth with water. Of course, if this were the World to Come, wouldn't all the dead be here and not just the recently murdered? As I say, I had hoped to see my mother. And I had heard, for instance, that one encounters Adam and Abraham and, very usually, the prophet Elijah, none of whom are

here. Otherwise, surely, they would have been called upon for speeches.

Perhaps Marek is right and all the promises were not promises, but lies. The memory of my murder is so distant that I have to remind myself that it happened at all. Still, I died, of this I'm sure. But somehow I survived and my body has been restored to me, as good as new, or very nearly. How can Marek explain this?

"An electromagnetic malfunction of our brain stems, perhaps," he says, tamping his cigar. "I couldn't really say."

Preposterous!

Still, it doesn't explain the absence of my mother, or of Ida and our child.

"Papa, does it matter where we are?" this from Hadassah. "At least we're together."

"That Marek," I say to her, under my breath. "What do you think? Was he truly a Communist?"

"Papa, don't," she says, looking away and refusing to answer. Has her sister sworn her to secrecy?

"You can tell your father," I say.

"No, Papa," Mirki cuts in. "He was never a Communist. Now are you satisfied?"

"Then why must he think like one!"

Our daughters and their husbands decide to stay up and move to the bar for late-night drinks.

Ester and I excuse ourselves and take their children up to bed. I hold Pola's and Sabina's hands, while Mirki's twins search through my pockets for hidden treasures.

"You won't find any," I say, but when they open their small, tight fists, each holds a round candy wrapped in a colorful wax paper.

"Well, well, well," I say. "I'm full of surprises."

"Only one each!" Ester snaps. "It's your bedtime."

She walks with Kubuś and Solek and Izzie. They escort her through the hallways like three gentlemen strolling with a dignitary through the streets of a capital city. They are talking, but quietly, almost formally. Their days of needing a grandmother's smothering sweetness have passed.

We arrive at their rooms, and after a thousand hugs and five hundred goodnight kisses, we leave the smaller ones in the charge of their older cousins and their siblings.

"Kubuś, you're oldest, remember," my Ester warns sternly.

"Goodnight, Zeyde," they call to me.

The hall is quiet.

I take Ester's arm and lead her to the lift, where the liftboy is drowsing on his stool. We allow him to sleep, his hands folded loosely in his lap, a bead of saliva on his chin.

Not knowing exactly what I'm doing, I pull the levers myself.

"Chaim, stop, stop. You'll get us killed!"

But after the initial jolt, the box moves fluently, although not to the proper floor.

"What are you doing?" Ester hisses, afraid to disturb the sleeping boy. "Chaim, you need to wake him!"

"Hold on, hold on," I say. How difficult can this be?

I have no idea which floor we're on. I look through the meshed door, to orient myself, and there she is. At least I think it's she.

Already in motion, my hands slip the levers into place, somewhere electrical connections are made, and our box rises, clanging, through its chutes, before I can get a second look.

"Ida?" I whisper to myself.

48

"I am sorry, Herr Skibelski, but there is no one here by that name."

"Then perhaps she is registered under her maiden name."

I am jumping from foot to foot before the registration desk, so nervous and excited am I at the prospect of seeing her again.

"In either case," the concierge says, closing his book, "I cannot give out the information you desire. Not all our guests wish to have their privacy disturbed. When you said her name was Skibelski," he digs at the wax in his fleshy ear, "I could at least assume she was a relative of yours, but now . . ." he hesitates.

"Kaminski is her maiden name," I plead.

"I understand that," he says, crossing his arms, "but I really cannot help you."

Before I can protest, a light is illuminated behind him and a buzzer sounds.

He turns back to me, looks me in the eye, although not unkindly.

"Excuse me, Herr Skibelski, I am called away to a staff meeting, where I will be for a goodly half hour."

He knocks a curled fist lightly against the registration book, twice.

"Our guests are registered in a rough alphabetical order," he says and he straightens his coat, pulling at his shirtcuffs, so that they are even. With a dismissive nod, he takes his leave.

"Thank you," I say, calling at his back.

"For what?" he turns imperiously.

"For nothing," I say, shrugging.

"Exactly, Herr Skibelski, exactly. For nothing," and he is gone.

Casually, I lean my arm against the desk. The lobby is all but empty. Here and there are couples, mostly men, conversing over nightcaps. I think of Markus and his friend Goldstein, talking in Vienna until dawn. A few waiters move sleepily from the bar to the lobby, ferrying drinks. No one is watching me, and so, with a tense nonchalance, I turn the thick registration book, so that it is facing me. Small tabs, embossed with letters of the alphabet, line the edge of its pages. I open the book to *K–L* and

scan with my middle finger through its various entries. *Kaufman, Klein, Kalovski.*

"Excuse me, sir," the voice is so close, I nearly jump, dropping the book from my hand, as though it were on fire.

A waiter holds his round tray vertically beneath his arm. There are circles of perspiration from sweating glasses dotting its cork surface.

"May I bring you a drink or some food?" he inquires. "Our kitchen will be closing shortly for the night."

"Thank you, no," I say, feigning insouciance. "I told a friend I'd meet him here."

"Very well, sir."

"This is the registration desk, isn't it?" I am overdoing it perhaps.

"Yes, sir, it is."

"I wasn't sure, you see. I thought perhaps I was at the wrong port."

"This is the registration desk," he says.

"Something must be detaining him."

"Your friend?"

"Certainly my friend," I say.

"I could have him paged for you."

"Paged?"

"If you wish."

"But that's not necessary."

"It's no trouble, sir. I'd be happy to do it."

I can't tell if he is merely being helpful or if he actually suspects me. I notice that my palms are sweating.

"Fine," I say. "Of course. A page. What an excellent idea."

At least this will get rid of him or so I think. I cross my arms and fold my hands under, concealing them.

The waiter removes a small notepad from his hip pocket, and a stubby pencil.

"His name?"

"Pardon me?"

"Your friend's name."

"You want my friend's name?"

"I'll need it for the page."

My mind goes blank. "Of course," I smile. The only name I can think of at the moment is my own. "Chaim Skibelski."

"Skibelski?"

"My friend's name is Chaim Skibelski."

"Very well."

He clicks his heels and bows slightly. Wheeling around, he traces his way through the lobby.

Quickly, I reopen the book and turn again to the K's to scour its pages for Ida's name.

"CHAIM SKIBELSKI!"

I cringe to hear my own name sounded through the crackling static of the hotel's antiquated amplification system.

"CHAIM SKIBELSKI! PLEASE MEET YOUR PARTY AT THE REGISTRATION DESK."

Katz, Kalzki, Kilzinski, Kalinski, Koslowitz. My fingers fly through the listings.

"CHAIM SKIBELSKI, YOUR PARTY IS WAITING FOR YOU AT THE REGISTRATION DESK."

What an idiot I am! This entire enterprise is nothing but foolishness! *Kalmanski, Karliner, Koslowitz.* To have slipped away from Ester with an excuse so lame I'm embarrassed to even mention it here—I told her that I wanted to inquire after the ingredients of a rum toddy I supposedly drank earlier in the bar, raving about the concoction at such length that I'm sure she either suspected my sincerity or thought me a complete ignoramus—only to be standing now at the registration desk, publicly sneaking through a forbidden book, while my name is blasted all about me in the air!

But Ida always had this effect on me.

I was a fool for her. I longed to marry her, at any cost. Of course, she hardly noticed me the day we were introduced, but from that day on, I couldn't get her from my mind. I was only seventeen, Ida fifteen. What was I doing, thinking about marriage? Still, I couldn't help it. Her father did business with mine, and there were many opportunities for me to see her, opportunities to impress her, although nothing I did seemed to catch her attention in the least.

My sisters whispered to me that Ida was desperately in love with

Oldak, a poet who also gave her violin lessons. If her father knew, or even her mother, my sisters told me, they would certainly disapprove, and there was no hope for the match. Despite his reputation, to Ida's prosperous parents, Oldak was a wastrel, a luftmensch. His passions were too fiery, his pocketbook too thin.

I myself wrote poems to her. Or at least I tried. Each morning I tore them to bits. There was nothing dashing or romantic about me. To her, I'm sure, I seemed less interesting than a clod of dirt, nothing more than the gawky brother of her friends.

Ida was seventeen when Oldak disappeared. It wasn't clear whether he had been arrested or whether he had fled to avoid such an arrest. No one knew, although we all suspected he was guilty of treasonable activities against the Czar's regime. Whatever the case, his disappearance had a disastrous effect on Ida. She ceased to eat. Her already pale face turned paler. Her high cheekbones became more prominent as her face grew thin. Her black eyes lost all their shining mischief.

Her parents were distraught and did not know what to do. Finally they decided that what their lovesick daughter needed was a husband. Surely it was time, none of us were getting any younger. A marriage would take her mind off politics and romance and the other useless pastimes with which they had unthinkingly indulged her.

Searching for a suitable groom, her father asked my father to inquire of me if I would consider marrying her. Taking me aside one

day, on our way to a mill, my father explained to me about Ida's hypersensitivity, her sadness, the difficulties of a poetic soul. A large dowry was being offered, he told me, so there would be at least some compensation.

"It's as easy to love a rich girl as a poor one, nu?" my Papa said.

As for me, I couldn't believe my luck and was beside myself with joy, although I managed to conceal it, asking my father blandly for details concerning where we would live, the two of us, and how we would manage. Even if Ida didn't love me, I thought, she might grow to. And at least now, there was a chance.

Ida, Ida, Ida Kaminski. Without my realizing it, my finger had stopped upon her name. How long I have left it there, absently tapping, I cannot say. Quickly, I jot down her room number, 519, on the back of an envelope with the Hotel Amfortas' letterhead printed on it in a raised blue script.

According to the registrar, she is traveling with her daughter, *my* daughter, the child we had lost.

49

Although Ida was not one for sweets, or so I remember, I purchase a box of chocolates and a dozen pale roses from one of the shops in the hotel's corridor of stores. For a moment, I consider buying a bottle of champagne, to celebrate, but perhaps it is too presumptu-

ous a gesture. It's been years since we've seen each other, not even taking into account the time that has passed since my death. I don't want to appear too pushy, too familiar. Neither do I wish to play the suitor, only to be rebuffed. I have remarried, after all, and am on holiday here with my family. Again, perhaps I didn't hear right or was not paying close enough attention when our Rabbis spoke of it, but I believe they said a righteous woman would be the footstool for her husband in the World to Come, if he were also righteous. But what of two wives? In any case, Ester will not be pleased.

I reach into the pocket of my nice new coat before realizing I have no money. The shopkeeper's eyes are tired, his face drawn. An old man in a velvet skullcap, he had been on the point of closing shop when I entered, but has patiently waited behind his stand while I shillyshallied over what to buy and what not, trying to recall Ida's tastes and the things that might please or displease her.

She was so careful about everything, the clothes she wore, the food she ate. No sweets or cakes but only wholesome foods. She wore a handmade dress to our wedding, one she had sewn for herself. And I was touched to see the care she took with it. After all, I was not entirely certain this was as happy a day for her as it was for me. She could have come in rags, for all I knew, carrying weeds.

"Is it possible to put this on my bill?" I ask the shopkeeper, abashed to find myself penniless.

"I didn't mean to rush you," he says deferentially.

"I'm new here," I apologize, "and I'm afraid I have no local currency."

"It's just tonight, you see, I have my appointment for the steam." This he says with an air of amused embarrassment, as though treating himself to the pampering steam were somehow shameful or unmanly.

"Of course," I say, "of course."

"It doesn't come too often."

"Forgive me for keeping you."

"But you needn't hurry," he says, rolling down his sleeves and removing and folding his apron. "We can put the amount on your bill, of course, Reb Skibelski." And he records my name and my room number into a small accounting pad he keeps next to his cash box, totaling my purchases and recording them there.

Through the meshed cage door of the lift, I see him turning out his shop lights. He has traded his velvet slippers for hard leather shoes and, holding his jacket over his arm, searches in his pants for the keys to lock his door.

The lift begins to rise.

The thought occurs to me that, since arriving here, I may actually have seen my daughter. And a thrilling, slightly disturbing thought it is. I have no idea if she is still an infant, she was only hours old when she died. Or has she grown up since her death? I haven't been dead long enough to know how these things work. In any case, there are many infants here, as well as many girls and young women, any one of whom could possibly be my daughter. Have we already spoken? Or

even caught each other's eye, never knowing whose face we were looking into? Probably not. Even if she is a young woman, nearly grown, would her mother really let her wander the hotel by herself, unchaperoned? Certainly not! At Ida's side or, if an infant, in her arms, it's likely it would be Ida I would have noticed first. After all, I recognized her in the hall, and even then, I saw her only fleetingly, not really for more than a glance. Still, I knew her immediately. If it was actually she. But why else would she be listed in the hotel register? Of course, it doesn't make sense that she registered under her maiden name. I can't say now whether she held a baby in her arms when I spied her from the lift. Funny the details one takes in, the things one doesn't. I'll invite them to breakfast for tomorrow and, there, introduce them to the others, Ida to Ester, Ester to Ida, my daughter to her half-sisters and half-brother. Marek will certainly have to swallow his words then, the rascal! With Ida's presence, who can doubt this is the World to Come, that we have, indeed, fallen into Paradise?

The lift attains the fifth floor. I'm perspiring so, I'm afraid I may have melted the chocolates. I should never have gripped them so tightly against my arm, and now I hold them away from the heat of my body. The lift doesn't stop evenly with the floor of the hall and I trip with my first step out. I struggle to regain my balance, feeling ridiculous, holding my chocolate box and the flowers for balance, like an acrobat falling from his rope. Behind me, I imagine I hear the liftboy smirk, although perhaps he merely coughed.

The hall is empty and, as I reach room 519, it occurs to me that I am a fool to have come this late. Surely, they are sleeping. There is no light beneath the door. Ida hated being woken in the middle of the night. Or was that Ester? Of course, who doesn't hate being woken in the middle of the night? I myself am not particularly fond of the experience.

Still, despite my misgivings, I rap softly, with a crooked knuckle, against the wood.

"Ida? Ida? Ida?" I whisper. "It's your Chaim."

It's impertinent, I know, but how long must I wait before seeing her?

I press my ear against the door. I cannot hear anyone stirring.

I rap again. The light tapping cracks like thunder inside the quiet hallway. God forbid I have gotten the wrong room! Or even another Ida Kaminski! Nothing about this enterprise is certain. I'm suddenly afraid of disturbing her neighbors. How humiliating to be caught here at her door and have to explain myself to them. What was I thinking?

Creeping back down the hallway, quickly, quickly, my flowers wilting and with my melted sweets, I reach the lift and summon it hurriedly, pressing the button on the wall.

Tomorrow is another day. In the light of morning, everything will be clearer.

I'll send a note to Ida first thing, a discreet inquiry as to her

situation, announcing my presence here. Was I really so boorish as to think I could burst in on her without even so much as a warning! It might have sent her into shock, seeing me. No, instead, I'll arrange to meet with her, accompanied by my family. That way, no one will be compromised, not Ida, not Ester or myself.

The liftboy rises out of nowhere, like an actor through a trapdoor on a stage.

What a sight I must be. Seeing this haggard fool before him, he hides his smirk behind his hand and conceals it with an artificial cough. So he did smirk! And he did cough! And why not? Who wouldn't laugh at me, a corpse courting his long-dead bride? Ridiculous!

I step in and stand beside him. He shifts his levers and, together, we ascend, side by side, to my proper floor.

50

Ester opens the door, barring my way. Her white and grey hair has fallen from its bun, framing her fleshy face with its thin wisps. Her robe has come open and her belly is big and white beneath her slip, with great swells of dimpled fat. With coarse, reddened hands, she pulls the folds of her robe across her granny's breast.

She turns her broad back on me without a word. But anything is better than looking into these angered eyes. Not knowing what to

do with them, I had leaned the flowers and the candy at a door across the hall with a note, "From a distant admirer," so at least I did not have to explain to Ester.

Moving past her, through the suite, I unbutton my vest and shirt, exposing my own large belly to the air. In the bedroom, I allow my pants to drop to my ankles, keys jangling in my pockets. Sitting on the bed, I remove my socks. For no reason at all, I place them on my hands. They look like puppets in a children's play about two monks. I take them off and throw them at the corner.

I dress in the nightgown and the tasseled cap the chambermaids left for me, when they turned down our bed. There's a fresh pair of undergarments inside the chest of drawers. I crawl under the covers and sit up, against the headboard, waiting for Ester. When she doesn't come, I call to her.

"Esterle?"

"A minute, a minute!"

I get out of bed and, in slippers, pad into the sitting room, where I find her, ironing out our wrinkled clothes.

My suit now hangs on a hanger without its recently acquired creases.

"Ester," I say. "What are you doing?"

"What am I doing?" she says. "What does it look like I'm doing?"

She throws her thick body into the work, moving the hot iron across a board that folds out from the wall.

"Leave it for the maids," I say.

"Go to bed, Chaim."

"But Esterle——"

"Now, Chaim, don't argue with me! Go to bed!"

She turns her dress over on the board and begins ironing its back.

I return to the cold bed and stare up at the ceiling. I'm more than half asleep when I feel the mattress tilt and sink beneath her weight. Without disturbing my covers, she pulls the blankets over herself and rolls her substantial body into mine. Brief kisses are clumsily exchanged between us in the dark. She pats my chest paternally and I am again asleep, baking in her heat.

5 1

I wake up, uncertain of the time. I reach for Ester but she isn't there. "Esterle," I call, sitting up. My first thought is she must be ironing again, or cleaning the silverware, but no light shines in from the other room. Running my hand across her sheets, I find that they are cold. I switch on the electric lamp and stare at my pocketwatch, which I have left on the small stand beside my bed, until my sleep-filled eyes will themselves to focus.

Four o'clock in the morning. Insane! Where could she be at such a time?

On the stand near her side of the bed I see the small blue appointment card. Handwritten on it in an elaborate cursive script are her names *Ester Blumenfeld Skibelski,* and the time of her appointment, *2:00 AM.*

Certainly, she should have returned by now.

I get out of bed, pulling the robe about my shoulders. Moving the fabric of the curtain, I peer through the window. It's completely dark outside. Even here, in the World to Come, there is no moon, and the meager starlight is obscured tonight by a thick skein of clouds. The lights from the hotel are ablaze, but as far as I can tell, no one is stirring or moving about on either side of the lighted windows. So much for Markus' cleaning crews working furiously through the night. I'll have to chide him about this in the morning, over coffee and hot porridge.

The hallway is empty as well. I quietly close my door, slipping the key into the pocket of my robe, and pad down the carpeted hallway in my slippers. I stop outside Sarah and Markus' door, rapping softly with my ring.

"Children? Sarah?" I whisper.

No one answers, but why should they? It's four in the morning. They're probably asleep or not yet returned from taking the steam. I'm about to turn away when I notice the thin line of light between the carpet and their door. I knock again and, again, receiving no answer, try the knob. It clicks softly.

"Hello," I call under my breath. "Markus? Sarah? Your door is un-locked. Children, are you here?"

But the rooms are empty, the beds in furious disarray. Every light in the suite is on. The windows have been left open, and a cold wind shrills, blowing the curtains in and out of the room. I cross to secure the windows. I'm disturbed to notice that all the luggage is gone. I unfasten the doors of the wardrobes, pull out the dresser drawers. They are bare.

I hurry from their rooms to Hadassah and Naftali's suite across the hall. It is empty as well. Neither is anyone in Mirki and Marek's suite, nor in Edzia and Pavel's. I'm running through the halls, like a madman, banging on doors. Every room, every suite in the long corridor has apparently been abandoned. "Hello!" I shout to no one. "Can anybody hear me?" Passing my reflection in the mirrored walls, I see a ridiculous man in a nightgown and robe running through the hallways, a cap's tassel dancing, like a sprite, upon his head.

How long have I been sleeping?

Not knowing exactly what I'm doing, I crank the levers in the lift and feel the floor give way beneath me with a sudden lurch. Corridor after corridor rise and disappear through the lift's meshed cage. Doors to suites have been left open, but no one is in the halls. "Jews!" I shout at every floor, unable to stop the lift. "Jews, where have you gone?"

The lobby, as well, is deserted. No one mans the front desk, the bars are closed and vacant. "Jews?" My voice pierces the emptiness

uselessly, resounding off the blotchy walls, from which the murals and tapestries have disappeared. In their places are unfaded squares of paint.

The winds spit in thick gales of snow through the heavy foyer doors. I manage to shut them, pushing with my bulk against each wooden half. Behind the front desk, the Direktor's office is locked. I pound upon the word *Private* stenciled into a small brass plate. "Herr Direktor!" I shout, but finally I have to kick it in. Inside, the bookshelves are bare and the desk drawers have nothing in them. I pick up the phone. There is no connection. "My God!" the words slip from my mouth.

Behind the front desk, I open the cash register. It contains nothing at all, no currency, no coins of any kind. The concierge's registry book, which I searched through only this evening, is new, its pages virgin and uncut.

"Rebbe!" I shout, running through the hotel's empty chambers. "Ester! Children!"

My words return to me, echoing off the atrium's curved ceilings.

I sit in the bar, slumped forward on a stool. Not even a bottle of vodka has been left behind! I try to think, but it isn't any good. I can't clear my head.

I cross my arms, perplexed, and am unnerved to hear, from above, a rumbling that seems to be coming from behind the scoured walls. Its scraping noises descend, growing nearer and louder.

"What's going on?" I demand of the air. I spring behind the bar

and leap upon the cupboard doors of a dumbwaiter, flinging them apart.

Inside, two lengths of rope move counterclockwise in measured intervals. I can hear the pulleys squeaking inside its chamber.

Slowly, as I watch, the box enters the cupboard, stuffed tightly with suitcases, many with colorful labels from various hotels. Several of their owners' names, written on tags, are familiar to me as they pass before my nose.

The box drops a foot or two at a time, in a stuttered descent.

There is someone else in the hotel.

5 2

I summon up the courage to search for the servants staircase, which I find near the laundry in the far eastern wing. The stairwell is pitch black and so I hunt through the laundry room, looking for a candle or a torch. Large vats filled with trousers and scarves send up curling lines of steam, as though they had been abandoned only moments before. Their waters are warm, the steam presses still hot. I nearly scald a hand touching their gleaming surfaces.

How easy it would be to return to my rooms, hurriedly dress and escape through the forests. This is the course a sensible man might take. A sensible man, I tell myself, would depart this queer

hotel at once, hesitating only long enough to randomly choose a direction in which to flee. But the anguish of separating again from my wife and my children will not let me take that path, no matter how sensible.

I find a small candle in a medicine kit tucked away behind a furnace. Lighting it, I cross the hall and enter the servants stairwell to follow the suitcases, down to the bottom floor.

53

My progress is slow. The passageway is narrow and the wooden, creaking steps are crooked and positioned badly in haphazard fashion. Perhaps the builder felt that here he could scrimp on a structure no paying customer would ever see. I press my hand against the dank, pitted wall, holding the candle with the other, near to my chest. The light it gives off is negligible. I inch my feet carefully from one step to the next, uncertain of the drop. A second step may fall six inches from the first only to be followed by a ten- to twelve-inch dip. Somewhere water drips with a purling tinkle. I sense that I am underground, although I have no proof of this other than the changing quality of sound and the dampening air.

At the edge of my small circle of light, a door appears. A heavy

door, made of dented metal and painted a muted puce. Dirty hand-prints mar its surface, and its paint has cracked and peeled. It no longer fits snugly into its frame, if it ever did, and so cannot be locked. I place my candle on a step behind me and, pushing with my shoulder, manage to force the enormous rectangle from its frame. It creaks and groans and opens. I jump across its threshold. It bangs behind me with a thundering boom.

The place, of course, is unknown to me, but I seem to be in a back storeroom of some kind. Huge bulging sacks of flour are stacked upon pallets and piled, against the walls, nearly to the ceiling. Large mechanical mixers and big dented brass tubs lay about in broken pieces.

Perhaps it is the kitchen.

At the far end of this room, through a screened doorway, a warm light glows. How reassuring it is to hear human voices and the sounds of people working! Churning machines, banging doors, tables being pounded. Instructions are shouted over the din and several conversations are going on at once. There must be a radio, for I can hear a waltz.

I peer around the edge of the wall of flour sacks. On the other side of the screened doors, several dozen men work beneath buzzing electrical lights. Bakers, by the looks of them. Each wears a white smock and a knotted kerchief. Puffy hats sit upon their heads, like large deflating mushrooms. At wide tables, they pound

great hills of dough with their fists and flatten them out with floury pins. Half a dozen bread mixers churn and grind. A big metal oven, nearly ten feet high, stands at the back of the room, giving off an exhaustive heat. One of the bakers opens its bottom door and throws in more wood. Inside, a red fire rages and glows.

"Hans, more wood!" they call out.

"Yes, sir!"

"Quickly, quickly!"

I edge closer, bending to hide myself behind a tall breadrack, wishing I had taken time to change my clothes. Ridiculous playing the spy in a flowing nightshirt and a tasseled cap, my legs bare and freezing. These slippers are not the most dependable of shoes, and every now and again, a frosty winter breeze blows beneath my hem, chilling my buttocks.

All the bakers appear completely bald beneath their fluffy hats. A flowing mustache is the only hair each seems to have. The oldest baker barks his orders, for instance, through a thatch of white snow. The first assistants wear ribbons of grey. The intermediate men smirk beneath luxuriant black bristles as thick as horse brushes. The apprentices breathe through mouths left open below scraggly fringes of down.

"The oven is hot enough, ja?"

Using a long metal stick, an apprentice unlatches and opens the oven's bottom doors. He feeds a fresh cord of wood into the raging

fire and checks its temperature at a circular gauge. Wiping wood chips from his hands, he nods affirmatively to his chief.

"Eins, zwei, drei, vier!" a middle baker calls out, and he and some of his fellows lift the apprentice and pretend to throw him into the fire. He kicks and struggles, but without strength, and this only makes the bakers giggle more. Finally they relent.

The head baker chuckles to himself, his eyes crinkling in delight.

"Much work, much work to do," he sings sweetly to the rest of them, lest in their merriment they forget their chores.

The other bakers puff their cheeks and blow out sighs. "Ach!" says one, crooking an arm against a tired back. "This work . . ."

"Enough of your complaints," his partner scolds. "We're almost done already for the night."

Not trusting the final preparation to any of his assistants, the head baker himself opens the oven's upper doors with the long metal stick. Picking up a paint brush and a bowl of melted butter, he layers the oven's inner shelves with a thick coat of grease.

"There will again be sweetness in the world!" he sings, pleased with the job he is making.

His assistants rush in to carefully take from him the bowl and the brush when he is through. One of the middle bakers offers him a towel and the head baker wipes his hands.

"Bring in the next batch," he orders, chuckling to himself.

"Hansel!" one of the middle bakers calls out, and he and his fellows move towards a large pantry. "Hansel, stick your finger out so

I can see if you are fat enough!" The others respond with much jovial laughter.

The men open the pantry door, disappearing inside.

"There will again be sweetness in the world," the head baker sings, rubbing his hands in glee.

54

The sweetish burning smells nauseate me. My stomach heaves into my throat. My hand slips and I lurch against a stack of precariously piled pots and pans, knocking them with a crash to the floor. The startled bakers look up from their work and with blinking eyes search in my direction. I scramble hastily to my feet.

"Madmen!" I shout, shaking my fists furiously, wanting to hit any who approach me.

"You're late," one of the middle bakers says, a little cross.

"Hand over your appointment card and we will begin," the head baker demands, turning his pointed belly in my direction.

The others move towards me, rolling up their sleeves. I pick up a hooked mixing oar to fend them off.

"My family," I say, "where are they?"

"Herr Jude," one baker says, "don't be such a fusspot."

"Not another step closer or I'll slice at least one of you!"

The mixing blade shines like a scimitar below the electric lights. I stand my ground, holding its point in the air between us. At a loss, the many bakers turn their mustaches in the direction of the head baker, who beams jovially at me, his cheeks like two fat roses, his eyes crinkling into merry circles of delight. His walrus mustache is as white as marzipan.

"Herr Jude," he says, a clucking laughter in his throat. "I must bake. Do you understand? Surely you don't wish to be the only Jew left in God's blue world?"

"Where is my family?" I say.

"Herr Jude," he demurs.

"I demand to know!"

His clear blue eyes look warmly at me over the tops of his flour-dusted spectacles. The glass is square without supporting frames.

"Gentlemen," he says to his staff. "Tell Herr Jude where his family is."

"They have taken the steam," says the first assistant.

"We have baked them," volunteers a second assistant and there is no mistaking the pride with which he says this.

"They have been in our ovens," says a middle baker, with equal pride.

"May we give you a guided tour?" one of the apprentices offers with a frank and open face, making all the others laugh.

I'm a risible figure, I know, in my nightshirt and my tasseled hat.

Nevertheless, as they come for me, I slash out with the mixing blade, slicing one of the apprentices across the bridge of his nose, tearing at his flesh. The young boy cries out in pain, bringing his hands to his face. My efforts produce a moment's hesitation in the advancing cohort. With new anger, the bakers trip over the spilled pots and pans I kick in their way. I send wheeled breadracks rolling towards them and limp hurriedly down the hallway, past the high stacks of flour sacks and back out the servants door. Someone has set off an alarm, it bellows and blares. I pause long enough in the dark stairwell to slide the mixing blade through the long handle of the door, forcing it into position and preventing it from being opened from the other side. Immediately, someone in the kitchen pulls against it, pounding on its hollow metal. The mixing blade works as a jam, but there's no telling if it will hold, nor for how long. My candle has long since burned out and I must scurry up the staircase in total darkness, holding the long hem of my nightshirt balled up in one fist so that I don't trip over it again and again. Because of the irregularity of the stairs, I bang my shins and knees anyway. At the top of the landing, I stick my head cautiously into the corridor. The alarm is sounding even louder here, on the hotel's second floor. Lights flash on and off. Excited shouts come from somewhere deep inside the ballrooms. Booted footsteps clatter through the hallways. Near the laundry room, I notice a small maid's pantry. The door, cut into the wall, must be no more than

two and a half feet in height. From the stairwell, I hear that the bakers have broken through my temporary jam and are now ascending the stairs. Their jovial threats, which they bark out in a teasing, pleasant way, echo through the chamber. With both retreat and advance cut off, I open the small maid's pantry and conceal myself behind a rickety fence of broom and mop handles, pulling the door to from the inside. There is no inner knob, only the quarter inch of screw that fastens the knob to the other side of the door's thin wood. The pantry is small. There is no way for me to get comfortable. I half lie atop water buckets and detergent bottles, terror filling my body with an electric pulse. Outside, the drumming of footsteps and a tangled chorus of voices pass my door at intervals. Whose voices and whose steps, I can in no way discern. Because, at some point, the sounds grow fainter and more distant, I assume my ruse has worked. Still, I daren't move or even attempt to shift my body, lest some slight sound reveal my whereabouts. A small duster has been poking me in the spine. One leg and an elbow tingle and grow numb. My mouth is dry and I am barely able to suppress the cough that is beginning at the bottom of my throat. The darkness, too, is intolerable. I wave my hand before my eyes, but can see nothing. My neck aches and when I move it, it pops audibly. If they've stationed some watchman or guard in the hall, the sounds from my neck would probably be indistinguishable from the creaking of the hotel walls. Perhaps he begins to slumber,

this guard, nearly as uncomfortable as I am. Perhaps he misses his bed. Perhaps he misses his wife and children. His feet grow numb and his mind begins to wander. He'd rather be farming. His cows need milking. He doesn't understand what he's doing, sitting here in an empty hotel, waiting for me to cross his path so he can shoot me and go home. I might as well let him. How long can I continue to hide in this way, folded in half, inside this little pantry? If I turn myself in, it would be from sheer boredom. I laugh at the idea, forgetting to stifle it. There's no telling the time. Could it possibly be morning? I imagine I hear birds singing. Surely it is morning. I can't hide forever. I'm only human. It would be different if I had a friend or a helper on the outside, someone who knew where I was, someone who brought me food or scraps of information, someone who could whistle a secret tune when it was safe to venture out. The man who is watching me, this watcher who I have thought about throughout this long night, perhaps he is a man whose secret sympathies lie with me. One can never tell. Perhaps he has been thinking of me as well at his station, during his long vigil. Maybe I could charm him into aiding me. Perhaps he will hide me in his barn, send his children out to me with food. They will cover me with hay if the soldiers come. At any rate, I'm suffocating in this little closet. I need to move. I cannot take it any longer. "All right, all right!" I shout. "Enough! I will surrender!" And with one foot, I kick open the cupboard door. The air rushes in. I am blinded by an intense glare.

Shading my eyes with a raised arm, I cannot look into the searing light of their one hundred torches.

They must have been gathering all night, these soldiers and vigilantes, outside my cupboard door. They have waited for me to reveal myself, so they may kill me at my most terrified. If I am crazed and animal-like, I will not fight back, and they can take greater pleasure in the killing.

I roll out of the cupboard, my hands raised, trying not to weep. As my eyes adjust, gradually, I am able to make out forms. I can barely stand on my numbed legs, they fall out from under me. I look around. The bright light of day spills through the many holes in the hotel's walls and roof. Nothing is left, but a dilapidated shell, no larger than a barn. There are no fine and fancy grounds, no stables, no greenhouses, no long palatial drives, no fountains and no pools. I'm standing in the middle of a green and sunny field. The air is fresh and fragrant. The birds, indeed, are singing. My eyes search the landscape, but can find no trace of snow. The earth is alive and green, the wind is cool, but pleasant. How long have I lain hidden in my little cupboard, cramped and twisted from fear? It must be early spring. I feel like a sleepwalker who awakens far from his home with no idea how he arrived here. I'm still wearing the hotel's nightshirt and its ridiculous tasseled cap. Across the field, a black shape catches my eyes, dangling from a tree.

"Rebbe!" I cry out, running to greet him.

But it's only my old suit, hanging on a branch, blowing in the

breeze. Sunlight dapples through the familiar pattern of bullet holes sewn irrevocably into its fabric. I find my old shoes, placed in a knothole in the tree's trunk. Pulling the nightshirt over my head, I knock the tasseled sleeper's cap to the ground. My naked belly is exposed and I'm dismayed to see that my old wounds have been restored. They are fresh and pustular, no longer covered with shiny scars. Gingerly, I raise my hand to my face and allow my fingers to probe the unnatural depressions and openings there and in the back of my head. I take the clothes off their branches and dress in my old shirt, my old jacket. I secure my old pants around my waist with my worn, familiar belt.

I sit upon the ground, beside the tree. I fold my legs and brace them with my arms.

THE SMALLER TO RULE BY NIGHT

55

I close my eyes and see only the ovens and their flames, their blue tongues licking across the bodies of my Ester, my Sarah, my Edzia, my Miriam, my Hadassah, my Laibl; consuming my sons-in-law and their children, Markus, Solek, Israel, Pavel, Pola, Jakob, Sabina, Marek and his daughters; devouring my town as well. Everyone I know, everyone I have ever known, has disappeared into the ash. I have torn my clothes and fallen to my knees, but my grief is insufficient. Were the oceans made of tears and the

winds of sighing, still there would not be tears enough nor sighs to assuage my crumpled heart.

Why was I given a body! I shout this to the Heavens. Why was I restored to my place at the head of my family! Why did You, in Your infinite wisdom and Your mercy, invite me to luxuriate in the Hotel Amfortas, delighting in its gardens and its lakes, only to see every dear thing billow up the kitchen stacks in black and stenchy plumes?

What are You thinking?

For Who Else could be behind such a monstrous affair, from which even the Rebbe's tender guidance couldn't spare me. No, it's impossible to doubt God's hand. Who but the Almighty could take a shabby house painter and, in a few short years, make him Chancellor of all Germany?

What difference does it make where I go? The sun burns, searing, above me. The long winds wail past. I wander through the woods, dour in thought, heading nowhere, walking in circles. The earth has vomited me out. I mutter to myself like a madman, fetid in her stench. If, as a child, I had been taken aside and told of the poisoned secrets my future hid for me in its coils, I would have fallen into a fever and died immediately.

Am I really expected now to carry on, without even a death to ransom me?

56

Deep in the forest, I find my rustic traveling sack hanging from a linden tree. The strap is looped across the gnarled blackened branch and the bag rocks slightly in the wind, as though a hand had placed it there only a moment before.

Who keeps playing these tricks on me?

Wearied by my own curiosity, nevertheless I cannot help but peer into the hanging bag. And what do I expect to find there? Money perhaps? Steamship tickets to Buenos Aires? Letters from a distant admirer?

I expect nothing at all.

And so I am not overly surprised to find, exactly as I had left them, the toy compass and the cracked telescope, which I rescued from beneath Ola's bed. (Dear little Ola, how happy and small her death now seems.) The family pictures are missing, but the ledger is neatly tucked inside. I open its covers and find that its pages have been singed and burnt. The remnants of my careful notes and drawings crumble and fall into the forest carpet. "Will it never end?" I shout this question to the trees.

I often speak aloud these days, sometimes shouting, often not, wishing I had no voice at all, that my thoughts might cease their feverish noodlings through my brain and disappear completely, folding in upon themselves.

57

I find there is no longer any need for food. I nearly choked upon the pine needle stew I made, more from habit than from hunger, near the river a day or so ago. I had to pick the nettles from my tongue, they clogged my gullet.

I had been dreaming of my mother's soup, her special recipe, that milky broth served steaming with a swirling ladle from the hotel's silver tureen. How I long to awaken to the smell of dark coffee and a bite of apricot blintz.

I sleep, beneath a crooked tree, my satchel for a pillow, and awaken in the night to hear weeping not far off.

Rising on an elbow, leaves sticking to my wounds, I strain to listen but soon the crying stops.

"Are you all right?" I call. The words are echoed back, as though I had addressed them to myself.

"Can you hear me?" I shout into the silence.

"Are you all right?"

But there is nothing. Only the sounds of the forest breathing. I brush the twigs and leaves from my face and lay my head again upon the satchel.

And then, unmistakably I hear the words *Chaim Skibelski, is that you?* cutting through the night.

I stand immediately. Searching the darkened forest paths and the pitch black silhouettes of trees, I cup my hands to my mouth and cry, "Yes, it's me! It's Chaim Skibelski! I am here!"

But I receive no further answer.

Soon the sky lightens and it is once again bright day. Overhead, an enormous aeroplane, larger than any I have seen, roars through the clouds, shaking the ground beneath my feet. It is long, enormously so, a blazing silver tube flashing in the early light. I thought an army must be approaching, such was the rumbling that preceded its exploding into view above my head.

58

Perhaps I can say Kaddish for myself.

This queer thought occurs to me as I loll about the ground beneath my tree. There is nothing else I have to do, nothing pressing. I've frittered away the last few days, stretched out in a tense indolence, feeling sorry for myself. Were it not for a suffocating grief that occasionally overtakes me, my days would have no shape at all, so encased am I in this hard, metallic gloom.

But why not? Why can't a soul recite the prayer for the dead over himself and somehow, on his own, effect his way into the World to Come? Our Sages teach us that if a person has no sons, a grown man may be hired to say the prayer on his behalf.

Why can't I hire myself?

True, I have nothing with which to pay myself, but then, on the other hand, I don't need much. Immediately, I agree to do the ser-

vice without charge. The merit of the deed will be all the greater for this small charity. *So why not, Chaimka?* I urge myself on. And in a twinkling, I am up, revived, and facing east. I feel as energetic as I can remember. I have nothing with which to cover my head, so I place my satchel across the top of my skull, holding its straps underneath my chin, drawing them together like the edges of a shawl.

"Yisgadal v'yiskadash sh'mei rabbaw," I chant. "Magnified and Holy be His Great Name!" I put my heart into it, davvening with all my soul. I've never prayed so fervently. "May the Maker of Peace in the high places make peace in the small places. For us, for Israel, and for all who mourn. And so we say, Amen!"

The *Amen* resounds through the forests, like a gun shot. I am stirred and awakened, anticipating in the next instant something momentous, something extravagant, something along the lines of Ola's ascension, but without the gaudy theatricals.

Nothing discernible happens.

I sigh.

Perhaps a subtle change has been effected, but it's very difficult to tell.

I sit again beneath the branches of my birch and return to the dawdling lethargy I had hoped to shake off with my prayers. Even if it were possible, not to mention permissible, to pray oneself into the World to Come, I know I do not have the stamina to keep at it for the required eleven months. My heart isn't in it, I have no minyan, and without the moon, who can keep track of the time?

I stretch and yawn and sadly contemplate the sky.

Surely by now, my sons in America know that we are dead. For isn't the war long over? Surely some survivor or witness has sought them out and knocked upon their doors. Clearing his throat and apologizing for his broken English, surely he has sat at their kitchen tables and been plied with honeycake and coffee by their wives. These he unhappily accepts from a sense of decorum, before telling them of our fates, my sons translating the Yiddish for their children. By now, surely, the coffee has grown bitter and the honeycake stale and tasteless on their tongues. Surely they have thought, with aching hearts, to pray the Kaddish that they owe me!

If not my sons, then *their* sons. Anyone over thirteen will do!

Or are the Gates of Heaven, God forbid, closed? Else, why has no one interceded on my behalf? Can Ester, whose soul I'm certain flew up the smokestacks to the highest realms of Holiness, not put in a good word for me? She, who harmed no one—surely they would listen to her! Will not our daughters plead for their father?

Or have they forgotten me?

How long must I wander, searching the larches for the Rebbe, craning my neck, calling up to the crows, "Excuse me, dear crows, but is my Rebbe there among you?"

"Who?" the birds squawk down, chattering, "Who who who?"

"Dear birds, my teacher, is he there?"

They address my inquiry to their companions, hanging like so

many black apples in the neighboring trees, cawing and clattering in their secretive tongue.

"Sorry," one bird calls down, translating. "No Rebbe here."

I have taken to walking at night, aimlessly. Too tired to sleep, I thrash through the woods, singing little melodies to myself, guided sufficiently by the stars not to break my neck. Sometimes I sit against a tree or near a lake and hold a small conversation with my-self.

"Chaim, Chaim, Chaim," I sigh.

"Oh dear, oh dear," I reply, the words escaping, almost like breath, from my mouth.

"And so," I begin a new point, but I lose myself in thought before I can continue.

59

Late one night, I inadvertently leave the borders of my forest and find myself upon a road that winds into a small provincial town. For no reason at all, I follow it past farmhouses and churches, over a small hill, across a narrow bridge, and am halfway down Kosciuszki Street before I realize that I am home. I am home. I am standing in my old town, on the outskirts of the Jewish quarter. I have to stop and gawk, so amazed am I to find myself in this old place. It's hard to say exactly what has changed. Everything seems different. The

roads are paved, for one thing, and, certainly, there are more cars parked along the streets. Before, Rosenthal and I were among the few private citizens with our own conveyances, but now they are everywhere, smaller and brighter than I remember, painted in all the hues of the color wheel, shaped as I have never seen them shaped before. There are no horse carts anywhere, that is new, and many of the old houses have vanished. In their places stand monstrous square buildings, nearly six stories high some of them, made entirely of glass. I get dizzy looking up into their mirrored surfaces. Familiar chestnut trees grow here and there, but the walkways, from the old bridge to the hospital, are lined now with rows of poppies, as red as a Bolshevik's black heart. Queer boxes dangle from wires stretched above the roads, but the red and green circles in them offer no real light, certainly not enough for a passerby to find his way across them in the dark.

Where once were shops, now people make their homes. Peering through their windows, I see them eating or talking with each other. They sit in groups around large boxes, on one panel of which a grainy photograph seems to be moving. It's very strange!

Even Ciacierski's café looks drab inside, with little to offer. A bored woman, the waitress, sits at a dingy table, painting her fingernails.

Most of the street names have changed. The old Talmud Torah sits now on Lenin Street, who could believe such a thing, opposite a large state building stretching from Wigierska all the way to

Ciesielska Street! Half of my own Noniewicza is gone, crushed beneath more of these glass monstrosities. It looks as if a new city has been dropped from the Heavens, quashing portions of the old town beneath it, wherever it fell.

It must be very late at night. I cross into my old courtyard. The apartments are dark, the residents are sleeping certainly, although through one window, I see a bright red dot glowing brighter and dimmer, brighter and dimmer, moving up and down in a curving arch. Someone cannot sleep and is smoking.

From the old Mintz apartment, I hear a series of tinny bells ringing and a groggy voice answers, "Hello?"

Is it possible each apartment now has its own telephone?

My old warehouse, with my office in it, is locked. Grasping the knob, I rattle the door, but cannot budge it. The timberyard is stacked full of wood. My gardens are in bloom. But who could be tending them? Big Andrzej is long dead, surely. Do his grandchildren work my gardens, assuming it was he and not I who planted them?

I bend to pick up a nice, solid rock, determined to shatter all the windows in the court, to see who might come running, when I notice the oddest thing. In a scattered pile of rubble is a stone, glowing faintly with a pale green light. Hobbling nearer, I touch it with my cane, dislodging it from its pile. It rolls upon the ground, crumbling into pieces and leaving a trail of glittering sparks. I hesitate to pick the curiosity up by hand. Perhaps it will burn me. There is a

similar rock about three meters further down the road. It too glows with the same tarnished gleam.

"What is this?" I whisper to myself.

Peering further into the gloom, I see they have been dropped, these rocks, periodically into the distance, as though someone were leaving a trail.

Despite my great fatigue, I follow the trail back into the forests, picking up the rocks and collecting them in my old traveler's sack. They are pleasantly cool, not hot, as I expected. And oddly, the sack grows lighter, not heavier, the more rocks I place into it. Although the silver glow emanating from beneath the flap is cool, it warms the part of my ribs I carry it against, like a cold fire, if such a thing may be imagined.

At one point, I must simply stop to gaze at the bulky collection, ripping aside the leather flap. Even the dust, crumbling off the rocks in speckled motes, is alive and burning with this greenish light.

I can't help laughing, I don't know why.

My trail ends at a small hut in the middle of the woods.

"Hello?" I call, knocking at its door, surprised by my own boldness.

I hear a shuffling and low murmurs and the scraping sound of someone walking on the other side.

The door opens a crack, revealing a narrow segment of an old face, its red beard, and one blue eye, glaring.

Seeing me, the eye softens and the door is further opened. An

old man, with stooped shoulders above his full red beard, pulls happily on his bristling sidelocks.

"Gut Shabbas," he says.

"Gut Shabbas," I stammer in reply.

"Gut Shabbas," he repeats.

"There is still Shabbas," I say, leaning into him, "even without Jews?"

"Who is it, Kalman?" a voice inside calls out, and the Hasid turns away from me to address his companion.

"It's Reb Chaim," he says simply.

"Reb Chaim?" sounds the voice, amazed.

"Nu, Zalman? He's arrived for Shabbas."

"Reb Chaim has arrived *here* for *Shabbas?*"

"Reb Chaim, please," says Kalman, turning again to face me, offering his limp and freckled hand. "Come in, come in. We're about to light the candles."

60

I can tell by the feel of his pale hand on mine that the man before me is alive. When I hesitate to enter, he tugs at me, circling his arm around my shoulder, pulling me inside.

"Welcome, welcome," he nuzzles my ear. "I have been calling you. Did you never hear me?"

He takes the bag from my shoulder and deposits it into a nearby corner, where, for a moment, it appears to float before settling onto the floor. The hut is dark. Through a window in its back wall, I can see that the sun is setting. The sight is troubling to me. Wasn't it deep night only moments before?

The other Hasid, Zalman, closes a book and rises from his seat. "Reb Chaim," he says, approaching me, both hands outstretched in welcome. "How long we have waited for you to cross our humble threshold!"

"And today of all days," says Kalman. "On Shabbas!" He returns from the sideboard with a silk skullcap for me to wear. "May our Merciful God be praised!"

"Praised be His Invisible Hand," says Zalman.

Despite their bristling, matted beards, nearly a foot wide across their wrinkled faces, the one silver with streaks of black, the other red with stains of grey, these two stooped Hasids seem as gay as children. From out the pockets of his long black coat, the one called Kalman removes a pair of short candles with an air of mischief, as though he were performing an impossible magic trick. He reveals the two sticks of wax, one in each freckled hand, and although I cannot explain it, my heart is pierced with sadness at the sight of his clownish pranks.

"Who shall light the Shabbas candles," he says, "and usher in a day of perfect peace?"

"You, Kalman, please."

They argue over the honor.

"No, Zalman, may the merit be for you."

"For you, I insist."

"Shall we ask Reb Chaim?"

"He is our guest, after all."

I demur. "I couldn't," I say, afraid my black mood will offend against their joy. "You're my hosts," I bow out, simply. "May the merit be for you both."

The two Hasids confer and agree to light one candle each, which they do, hiding their eyes behind their translucent hands until the blessings have been said. They gaze upon the flames as though upon the first small lights of Creation, tears welling in their eyes.

"Remember how my Chaya and your Chana used to light the Shabbas candles together?" Kalman wipes his cheek against his sleeve.

Zalman stiffens. "You mean *my* Chaya and *your* Chana," he says.

Kalman squints.

"I was married to Chaya. You, Kalman, to Chana."

"God forbid I should not remember my own wife, God forbid!"

"We married sisters," Zalman explains to me.

"Not to mention my own sister-in-law you're suggesting I forget?"

"They were twins." Zalman explains. "Identical."

"Zalman, they were fraternal!"

"God forbid I don't remember!"

"He doesn't remember, Reb Chaim, it's been so long."

Zalman shrieks. "It's you, Kalman, who has forgotten who doesn't remember!"

"One of us doesn't remember," Kalman says kindly, making peace, "but which one it is, to tell you the truth, we can no longer recall."

It's understandable. My head is swimming. If they move too quickly about the room, I myself forget who is who, and must wait until one addresses the other by name in order to reestablish their identities.

"But enough!" says one. "We're driving our poor guest mad."

"Reb Chaim," the other clucks his tongue. "Sit, sit, sit."

They escort me to a chair in the middle of the room. The table, with its three chairs, is simple, hewn from pine. The dark hut is sparse, its dirt floors swept clean. In one corner a pallet is covered with straw, on top of which is a jumble of blankets. Here, I assume, the two must sleep. Below one window, a small shelf is stuffed to overflowing with holy books. Near the other window, a battered grandfather clock ticks with a slight irregularity.

The Hasids return to the table, the one carrying a bottle of wine, the other a silver Kiddush cup. The wine is poured, the blessings recited. The evening is now sanctified. Each offers the others a toast and good health, and the two Hasids drink.

"Reb Chaim?" says Kalman, lowering his cup from his lips. "You are not drinking?"

"There is something wrong with the wine perhaps?"

I move the glass away from my plate, gently, with two fingers at the base of its stem.

"Perhaps you have not realized," I reply, "but my wounds were fatal. It's gracious of you not to have said anything or drawn undue attention to them. But I understand you could not have helped noticing."

The two Hasids grunt, looking at the table. They nod their embarrassed assent.

"As a dead man, it is, of course, impossible for me to drink."

"But today is Shabbas," says Kalman, peeking over the hedge of his beard. "Today, even the dead may eat and drink."

Among their Hasidic pieties is the quaint notion that the dead, on the Sabbath, are released from their torments and may feast. Our more rational philosophy never concerned itself with such fairy tales. And yet, despite everything, here I am, stuck in a kind of netherworld I never anticipated and so out of politeness and from a measure of curiosity—after all, if I have learned anything since my death, it is that one must never grow accustomed to the seeming laws of one's existence, for as soon as one does, they are certain to change—I raise the cup to my lips and drink. The wine is inordinately sweet. My esophagus tightens around it. We toast each other again, raising small thimbles of Russian vodka and my empty belly is roused by the liquor's fiery warmth. Tears well up in my good eye. The three of us are moved to exchange moist kisses. We step into

the cold evening breeze to wash our hands at the well and return in silence to the table for bread and then for soup.

"A simple meal, a simple meal," says either Kalman or Zalman, who can keep them straight?

The steam from the soup rises to fill my nostrils. Despite its tasty aromas, I sink back into my chair, utterly morose, my appetite dwindling away like blown straw. How can we eat and drink when so many have perished? I don't care if it is the Sabbath!

Carefully, the Hasids blow upon their raised spoons and I find I cannot look at them.

6 1

"And so," I say, addressing my hosts, my hands folded neatly before me, "how is it you two managed to survive?"

Despite my pleasant tones, something of the bitterness I am feeling towards them has broadcast itself through my speech. The mood in the room instantly sours. Kalman lowers his spoon and looks to Zalman for help. Zalman pushes away his bowl, waving a hand over it.

"Reb Chaim, forgive us," he says. "We don't mean to make you feel in any way . . ."

"Aggrieved," suggests Kalman.

"But there are worse things . . ."

"Worse things, oh yes."

". . . than not surviving."

They nod gloomily and, helplessly, I regret my words.

"Forgive me," I whisper, ashamed of myself. "It is, of course, wrong for me not to rejoice that Jews still walk the earth."

"In the pitch black of night!" Zalman says bitterly, knocking his bread plate halfway across the table.

"Zalman, let us not speak of it on Shabbas," his brother-in-law hisses between tight teeth.

"Shabbas! And how do we even know this is Shabbas?"

"We know."

Zalman tears the napkin from his chest. "Without a moon?"

"We know very well without a moon. You know what the holy books say."

"Yes, I know what the holy books say!"

"That a man lost in a wilderness without a calendar may count the days, celebrating Shabbas on the seventh," Kalman wags his finger at his brother-in-law's face.

"Still, it is not the same!"

"It *is* the same," insists Kalman.

"It's not!"

"And if it isn't, we can talk about it later. After Shabbas. But not today."

"Reb Chaim," Zalman continues, ignoring his brother-in-law's

pleas. "You have perhaps heard of two Hasids who pulled the moon from the Heavens?"

The story comes back to me. Vaguely, I recall it. A German head talking, a little Polish girl's bedtime tale, or was it one of the Rebbe's cryptic allegories, the sort of story he relished telling after the Third Meal, the sun sinking, with its light, from the sky.

"I have heard of such things," I say guardedly. "Who knows if they are true?"

"We know," says Zalman, "because we are those men."

Zalman and Kalman cannot avoid looking at each other, sheepishly. So similar are their faces—big shaggy beards beneath fur streimels—I have the impression of watching one man encountering himself in a mirror.

"What we have done cannot be undone," says Kalman, sucking on the red rectangle of beard beneath his lip.

"What my brother-in-law has said," Zalman tells me in a lowered voice, as if in strictest confidence, "is not altogether true."

But, of course, his brother-in-law is sitting right across from us, hearing every word.

"What did you just say?" he screams.

"Kalman, control yourself!"

"On Shabbas, you dare to speak of such things!"

"But it may not *be* Shabbas!" Zalman rails.

"It would be Shabbas, if you'd only agree that it is!"

"But I don't feel in my heart that it is."

"Because you keep acting as if it isn't."

"Is the rest of the world observing it today? How are we to know?"

"Please, Zalman, things were going so nicely," Kalman murmurs. "We have a guest."

"Reb Chaim, all I am implying," says Zalman, giving in to his brother-in-law's wishes, "is that I have perhaps found a way to return the moon to the sky." He raises his hands, as if to erase his words. "More than that, I will not say until Shabbas has passed."

I sigh, regretting that I ever knocked upon their door. How the living spin their plans and schemes, unaware of their utter futility!

"Now," says Kalman with relief. "If everyone agrees, I think perhaps it is time to sing."

And they drone their wordless melodies, these two Hasids, deep into the night, until finally their voices crack and I am allowed to sleep.

62

I spend the Sabbath hating them bitterly. Simply for being alive when I and my family are not. Where do they find the gall to persist in their petty lives? Choosing a hat, locking a door, corking a bottle of wine. The care they take over each and every pointless detail. It sickens me. My food grows tasteless in my mouth. I cannot swallow

it. I look across the table into their beaming faces and see, instead, my own children's faces and the faces of my grandchildren, and even *their* children's faces, faces now that will never be born.

Many, many worlds have been lost, not simply my own.

As the Hasids renew their interminable singing, I can't help longing for the delightfully quiet Sabbaths we used to spend in our own home in our courtyard on Noniewicza Street. Ester lighting the candles, my girls setting the table, everyone rushing around, rushing around, freshly washed, hurrying, hurrying, as though our very lives depended on having it all prepared before nightfall. Often, my father joined us, a widowed old man, sitting at my right, his white shirt starched beneath his frayed black coat, his yellowed beard newly combed and washed. As a boy, I hid behind my mother's skirts, fighting not to have him make the blessings on my head. How big they were, these giants, my father with his coal black beard, my mother with her strong hands tearing at my frantic arms, pulling them, like garden worms, from around her tree-trunk legs.

Enough, Chaimka! Enough! Oh, how they'd shout at me!

And now, instead, I'm forced to listen to these Hasids noisily pounding the table with their soft and delicate fists. So much noise from such soft hands!

I can't help longing for my solitude and my forests, for my bed of nettles and twigs.

63

Immediately following Havdalah, before Kalman has had time to resign himself to the new week and its work, and as I, myself, clear my throat in order to tender my perfunctory thanks and make my escape as quickly as possible, Zalman springs from the table and bounds ferociously over to the little bookcase with the speed of a man half his age.

Irritated by his brother-in-law's abrupt dismissal of the Sabbath Queen, Kalman begins to protest. "But Zalman!" he shouts, still holding the braided Havdalah candle in his fist, smoke rising in curling lines from its many wicks.

I make a futile attempt to reiterate my gratitude and my farewells, but neither of them will listen to me.

Bending at the knee, Zalman finds the book he is searching for and returns with it to the table. With a long finger, he points into an open page.

"Reb Chaim, here is something you must see!"

"Zalman!" snaps Kalman. "Why are you rushing him so! Let him sit, let him sit. I'll bring the schnapps."

"Reb Chaim, Reb Chaim!" Zalman taps his finger impatiently against the page.

Wearily, I move to him and look where he is pointing.

"Well?" His eyes burn, gauging my response.

Although the Hebrew characters are familiar, it is a book I have

never seen. From the odd diagrams that litter its margins, I conjecture that we are gazing into the pages of some obscure and perhaps even dangerous tract. I lift my eyes, meeting Zalman's. He raises an eyebrow. Its bristling hairs arc in the middle.

"You've assumed correctly, Reb Chaim. This is one of the most secret of our most secret books."

I don't know what to say. For whose benefit are they staging this ridiculous melodrama? Surely not for mine.

"Schnapps anyone?" Kalman enters from the back, a bottle in the crook of his arm, carrying three glasses between his splayed fingers.

Zalman ignores him and I look longingly towards the door.

"By dedicating myself exclusively to its study for the past fifty years," Zalman says, demanding my attention, "I have been able to translate it into a system of coordinates, whereby I have produced . . . this map."

With a flourish, he removes a large scroll from behind the bookcase. Placing the holy book to one side, he unrolls the heavy vellum and pins its corners to the tabletop.

Resisting the urge to run, quickly, through the doorway and back into the forests, I fold my arms behind my back, nod my head, and glance politely at his scroll.

It is a map like no other I have seen.

There are no sketched representations of topographical features. Instead, what I see, laid out cleanly before me, resembles an unwieldy mathematical equation. Long lines of numbers cross the

sheet at random angles. Unsteady columns of numerical values lean precariously in every quadrant. Great curving wheels of words whirl and turn in compressed spirals. Two-headed arrows crisscross everything in waves. The phrase *patterned energy* is underscored with violent blue hatchings. Zalman seems to have constructed a code using different colors: black, purple, violet, yellow, orange, amber. At the center of its four edges, he has sketched, in lurid detail, the heads of horrible demons, stiff tongues thrust forward through mocking grimaces, their eyes ablaze, and below each, the legend: *Beware! Beyond this boundary — madness!*

"I don't understand," I say, perplexed.

"Of course not," says Zalman.

"Me neither," Kalman chimes in politely.

"There are days I wake and have forgotten everything myself. On such days," says Zalman, "I must purify myself through prayer and fasting and ritual immersion."

"Sometimes ten a day," Kalman interjects.

"Only then does my work again begin to make even the barest of sense to me."

"He prays all day, all night. 'Zalman,' I say to him. 'Eat a little something. You'll grow faint. It isn't healthy.'"

"Here," Zalman points to a large X with his bony middle finger. Black hairs curl in a wiry riot around its knucklebone. "Beneath the portion of earth represented by this part of the equation lies the

moon, buried, or so I estimate, some seven to twelve meters deep. It's taken me fifty years, but I've found it, I'm sure."

"With my help," Kalman adds quietly, eyes brimming with pride.

"But why haven't you set out to retrieve it?"

Zalman's head drops. He folds his arms and stares glumly at the floor.

"We were given strict orders to wait."

"Whatever for?"

"Why, for you, Reb Chaim."

For me?

"It was the Rebbe's final instruction to us."

" 'Do not leave this hut until after Chaim Skibelski has arrived.' "

"He was very strict, very clear."

" 'Do not leave this hut until after Chaim Skibelski has arrived.' "

"Thank you, Kalman, I think that is sufficient."

My anger rises. "But he could have told me to come here in the first place. My house is not five versts away!"

"You can be sure," says Kalman, unsuccessfully hiding a grin beneath his mustache, "if the Rebbe said to wait, it was with a purpose."

"Don't be angry, Reb Chaim."

"You think we didn't wonder for fifty years why we were required to stay in this hut?"

"But how did you eat, how did you gather food, if you were forbidden to leave?"

"Baskets of food were left on our doorstep."

"Wine and other drinks, we found at the well."

"And besides," says Zalman, "we have no exact idea where we are. Without a compass, this map is utterly useless."

64

They have lived together in solitude for more than fifty years. Is it so unusual, after such time, that neither has to speak to make his thoughts known to the other? Still, the private look they share when I tell them, "I have a compass," is alive and brimming with relief. And although I sense that they are not surprised at this turn of events, the pleasure they take in it has caught them, to some degree, unaware.

"Zalman!" Kalman strokes his red-grey beard, pleased as a cat. "Imagine that! Reb Chaim has a compass."

Zalman's hands hug one another with anticipatory glee. He pulls at his vest and coat, as though preparing to face a dignitary.

"I'm afraid it's a mere child's toy," I say, searching the hut for my bag and finding it tucked away in the corner by the bookshelf. "One of my daughters shared it with a friend. But it works. Or at least I think it does."

I pour the contents of the bag onto the table in search of the little toy. The pile of rocks glows like a small mountain of tarnished silver.

The compass and its companion, the telescope, I find at the bottom of the sack. Wiping the gleaming dust from its glass face with my sleeve, I offer it to my hosts.

"Here," I say. "You may keep it."

"These stones," says Zalman, but his speech fails. He stares at the rocks in silence, ignoring the compass I hold out to him.

"Where did you find them?" Kalman finishes their sentence.

"They seemed to lead here from my old house. I followed them to your hut. As though they were a trail."

Zalman has to sit. Pensively, he pinches his nose between his thumb and the middle knuckle of his index finger.

"All these years . . ." he says. "All my work . . . and I never imagined this day would come . . ."

"Exactly as the Rebbe has foretold!" Kalman addresses this comment to no one in particular, raising his hands in a gesture of helpless amazement.

"You see, Reb Chaim," Zalman's eyes swim in tears. "Oh, but you have no idea."

"They're moon rocks," Kalman is barely able to whisper these words.

65

Zalman slaps his knee and stands. "We must begin tonight!" He rolls his map into a long cylinder and binds it with a blue silk ribbon. Kalman removes a silver key from a chain around his neck and, with it, opens the lock on a moldy wooden chest. From here, he extracts several long shovels and pickaxes.

"As for food," says Zalman, "we will have to do with what God provides for us along the way."

They help each other out of their long Sabbath coats and into short traveling jackets, exchanging their round streimels for black fedoras, which hang on pegs near the door. Each places the other's hat first upon his own head, before realizing his mistake.

When they turn to me, their faces are alive with anticipation and adventure.

"Gather your things, Reb Chaim," Zalman gestures to the pile on the table.

"What's this?" Kalman holds up the collapsible telescope.

"A child's toy as well. Unfortunately, it's cracked."

"Bring it, bring it all the same," calls Zalman, already out the door. "You never know what might come in handy."

"But I'm not going," I say.

I sit at the table. Zalman must come back through the door, his brow in a knot. "He's not what?"

"You're not what?" Kalman asks, smiling as though at a joke he does not understand.

"I'm not going."

"He says he's not going."

"Kalman," Zalman glowers at me from the threshold. "Explain to him that he must!"

Kalman brings his soft fist to his lips. He coughs to clear his throat. He rubs his hands together and searches the ceiling as if looking there for his words. "Reb Chaim," he scratches his head. "But how may I put this?"

"Get on with it! Get on with it!" barks Zalman. "We haven't the time for this nonsense!"

"You haven't the time!" I shout at him. "You haven't the time! You spend the war safe in the lunar atmosphere while the rest of us are dying! For that, but not for this, you had the time!"

Zalman crosses and uncrosses his arms. Kalman places his hands meekly in his pockets.

"Don't act so pious," I sneer. "It was thanks to your own greed that the moon was lost. Don't think I haven't heard the story!"

"Reb Chaim," Kalman smiles sweetly, as though I were a village idiot who barely understood the intricacies of his shoelaces. "Fifty years ago, when he brought us to this hut, the Rebbe assured us that although we would eventually find you, we would have to wait a long, long time. We were young men when we came here. That

was fifty years ago. The Rebbe took me aside, Reb Chaim, and this he said to me: 'When Reb Chaim arrives, he will hate you bitterly. He will pretend to enjoy the Shabbas, but all the time he will be longing to get away.' He said, 'He will give you the compass, but he will refuse to accompany you. However, you must insist upon it. You must tell him there is no choice, much is at stake, including the World to Come.'"

"The World to Come!" I sit thickly in my chair. I, too, cross my arms, not wanting to listen.

But Kalman persists. "The Rebbe authorized me to say on his behalf, 'Do not despair, Chaimka. Soon everything that needs to will make sense.'"

He bends so I may look into his face.

"Reb Chaim," he tells me, "the Rebbe said we should be happy."

So what am I to do? Bury myself in their bed, hide beneath its straw? For how many days and to what end? If the Rebbe insists, who am I to argue?

I gather up the compass and the little telescope and leave the moon rocks shimmering in their pile upon the table. Looking around the tiny hut, I kiss its mezuzah and am again in the forest, following these two madmen to the moon's hidden grave.

66

We march through the forest, our shovels and push brooms and pickaxes held high against our chests. A clanking toolbag dangles on a strap from Zalman's shoulder and he has tied two metal buckets to his waist with a rope. Kalman pulls a large vat of seawater on a wheeled pallet. The liquid rolls precariously from rim to rim, but so far has not spilled. He totes, as well, a long ladder on his shoulders, his head in the empty space between two rungs. Everything they need they seem to find along the way, hidden here and there, among the trees. They have made me responsible for a tan canvas bag stuffed with pulleys and winches. This I secure across my left shoulder and my rustic's bag across my right. The thick rope, of which I am in charge, I keep in a coil around my waist.

Our progress is slow.

Periodically, Zalman unrolls and consults his map, comparing its numbers to the dial on our compass, adding figures to his equations with a short red pencil. At these times, Kalman and I unburden ourselves of our load and sit upon tree stumps, the silence broken only by Kalman's explanations of Zalman's activities. These he whispers into my ear, but because he keeps his voice so low, out of fear of disturbing his brother-in-law, I have no idea what he is saying. Rather than asking him to repeat himself and risking a disturbance, I nod, as though I have understood, and direct my attention, in an

interested manner, towards Zalman's back. This seems to please Kalman who will once again wrap himself in a snug and tight silence, leaving me in peace.

Zalman's calculations may take hours to configure. At other times, he has only to scan the map, referring quickly to the compass, and we must rise almost as soon as we have settled in, gathering our heavy gear and marching off, our buckets and shovels, our pulleys and winches clanking noisily. We must sound like a trio of overburdened knights to anyone who might hear us.

That my old and broken body is capable of carrying such a frightful load is an astonishment to me. I barely make use anymore of my cane. Still, I keep it, if only for balance and as a reminder of who I once was. Also it's good for cracking open walnuts, which I do for Zalman and Kalman, when they are forced to eat.

Sleeping does not seem to have a place on our itinerary. Zalman's concentration is furious, intimidating. Staring hawk-like through the gnarled trees, somehow he is able to discern in their shadowy groves our necessary path. Neither Kalman nor I have the nerve to approach him in this state with a request as self-serving as sleep.

And so we stumble on, through the forests, until our drowsiness, pulled down by its own weight, turns into an alert dreaming, in which our bodies seem to function on their own. My sense of time is, once again, unreliable. The night lasts forever and we march deeper and deeper into it.

Eventually, we come to an empty forest road and are about to cross it, when a colossal logging truck comes barreling around a hill, heading straight towards us. Zalman extends his arm in front of Kalman and me, knocking against our chests, preventing us from entering the road, where without question we would have been smashed.

The truck blares past, its harsh headlights shining in conical beams, its open windows emitting strange sounds, wild and pounding, with chaotic rhythms, as though the driver were beating a club against the interior of his cab.

"Techno-rap," Kalman whispers knowledgeably.

"During the war," he explains, "I built a small radio out of spare parts, so we could listen to reports of the battles. It still works and I like to keep up."

I have no idea what he is saying. But, again, I nod and grin and redirect my gaze from his face to the rear of Zalman's head. Behind my own head, I hear him sighing, content that he has laid one more mystery to rest.

Zalman checks the way, removes his arm as a barrier, and allows us to advance across the road and back into the thickness of the trees.

67

"At first, we could not believe our good fortune," Kalman murmurs this to me. "Of course, before that, we had argued over who was to blame. And naturally, we blamed each other. 'If I hadn't listened to you,' he shouted. 'We'd be dead in the forest!' I shouted back."

Why must everyone I meet tell me his story? It's as though I wore a sign across my brow: Share with me the tedious details of your life!

He continues. "But, Reb Chaim, the air is so thin, so thin up there, it's difficult to argue. You can't shout. There's nothing to fill your lungs. And also, the beauty, Reb Chaim, the beauty! You can't imagine! It leaves you wanting to be quiet. There are vast riverways of stars flowing through the Heavens. Even now, it's impossible for me to speak, just thinking of it. That I should merit seeing such splendor!"

And for many steps, he does, indeed, remain silent. Eventually, his rapture passes and the tale begins anew.

"Our boat was pulled, soon enough, into the lunar tide. We arrived and settled in next to a monstrous crater. And what should we find there, covering its icy surface?"

Before I can guess, he has answered the question himself.

"A hundred pots of silver! A hundred? No, many thousands!

"We can't stop congratulating each other, jumping up and down, each praising the other for his courage, for his great courage, in

seizing the boat, which we anchor securely to the moon with a thick and sturdy rope.

"It took many nights, Reb Chaim, many cold nights, to gather all the silver. There was so much of it and it was freezing, I tell you! We had to wear gloves just to handle it, piling each little potful into the boat, stacking it so high, so high, that when Zalman and I stepped back into it ourselves, it was too heavy. The boat started to sink and, before we could even cut the rope, we had pulled the moon from the Heavens."

68

"But that's impossible," I say, not ceasing from my walking.

"Impossible? Of course," says Kalman, giggling behind me. "Nevertheless, it's true."

"The weight of the silver, which was originally supported by the moon, even when transferred to the boat, couldn't cause the moon to sink."

"The moon doesn't sink," Kalman corrects me. "The boat sinks."

"The boat sinks, all right. But it shouldn't pull the moon down with it, since the moon is able to sustain the silver's weight. And although the silver is transferred to the boat, its weight doesn't increase. There is no added weight."

"Except for our hearts, Reb Chaim. How heavy they grew,

knowing the trouble we were causing, pulling the moon from the sky."

He shifts the ladder on his shoulders.

"That is something your mathematics and your astronomies cannot measure."

69

According to Kalman, the two of them landed back in the forests, embarrassed over what had happened. They cut the rope that tethered the moon to their small craft and watched, in dismay, as the boat rose with all their silver, and the moon remained exactly where it had fallen.

"We tried forcing it back into the skies, but, of course, for that, we did not have sufficient strength."

Still, neither considered abandoning the orb. Instead, they tucked their sidelocks behind their ears, spat upon their hands and, with their shoulders, began pushing the giant ball along the winding forest paths.

They were again alone in our dark and terrible woods, but now with a large planet glowing conspicuously through the pleaching trees.

Near dawn, when the moon was as white as a dish, they chanced upon an abandoned farm, east of the Soviet border. Huffing and

puffing, they rolled the moon into the tall barn, closing its high, flat doors behind them.

There, they concealed the moon beneath as much hay as they could gather and, for the first time in what felt like a month, they slept. Each night, however, the moon grew smaller and smaller. This so distressed the Hasids that they couldn't stay hidden beneath their own haystacks, but crawled out obsessively to check upon its progress. They couldn't lie to themselves: the moon was definitely waning. And finally it disappeared.

The three nights that followed were difficult ones, emotionally wrecking for the Hasids. How they fretted and fussed, tearing at their beards, wailing for mercy! Still, as terrible as these nights were, they were nothing compared to the fourth night when the moon failed to reappear. The Hasids raged madly through the barn, searching the cracks in the floor for even the smallest of crescents.

Nothing could be found. They held each other and wept.

The earth was dark and they had lost the moon.

7o

Can it possibly be true, Kalman's story? On the surface of things, I have every reason to doubt him. Perhaps they pocketed the silver for themselves and are hoping now to recover it. Why should I believe their story? Still, he's a trustworthy sort, this Kalman, and a fellow

Jew besides. It's forbidden for him to deceive me. Not that it hasn't been known to happen, one Jew lying to another, we're only human, after all, but, still, what's forbidden is forbidden. Plus, he's a Hasid, he's taken on more than the Law requires. He'd be cutting his own throat, lying to me.

Along with the two bags and the shovel and the broom I am forced to carry, these thoughts weigh me down until each footstep is more difficult than the last. I am about to insist upon stopping for the night, when our clanking trio emerges into a vast and open field. The light from the stars, no longer obscured by foliage, shines on the grass so clearly that every blade seems to stand out against its own shadow. Checking the field's mathematical correspondences, Zalman allows himself one small syllable of satisfaction: "Ha!" He drops to his knee and, with a spade he has carried on his belt, over-turns a swallow tuft of earth.

He sifts the black dirt through his fingers, raising his smudged hand towards Kalman's eager face.

"Kalman, tell me, what do you see?"

A repressed cry of joy manages to free itself, if only momentar-ily, from Kalman's throat.

"Exactly," says Zalman, "exactly." And again, he picks through the moistened loam. "Now, Reb Chaim, look." He extends his palm to me. I step closer. He holds a small portion of the fallen night, or so it appears, so many silver motes are gleaming in the blackened dirt.

I raise my gaze from his flat palm to his hawk-like face. Behind

the wild and now unruly beard, his black eyes burn even more wildly.

There will be no sleep this night, I sadly tell myself.

Zalman slaps his palms, one against another, cleaning them, returning the dirt to the ground. He gives me a bracing chuck on the shoulder, as though he has read my thoughts. With Ola's compass in hand, he counts seventy-seven large paces, moving to the center of the field. Remembering the small telescope, I bring it from my traveler's sack and watch him through its fractured lens.

"What's he doing?" Kalman breathes impatiently on my neck, pulling with both hands on his reddish beard.

Consulting the compass, Zalman faces all four directions, one after the next, before settling on one. He spits into his palms and raises the pickaxe high above his head. Bracing his legs, he brings the axe down, cutting into the earth.

"What's he doing now?" Kalman jumps from leg to leg, squinting into the distance.

"I'm not sure," I say.

"Let me see, let me see!" Unable to stop himself, Kalman pulls the lens from my good eye.

"Ah yes ah yes I see I see," he says, all in one breath, before returning the spyglass to me.

I once again peer through the little tube. Zalman is on his knees, with a mallet, pounding pegs into the ground. He reorients himself

with the compass, until he is sure he is facing our direction. He waves his long arm and motions us to join him.

What are we to do? Kalman and I collect the equipment and struggle with it to the center of the field.

"Kalman, Chaim!" Zalman shouts, returning a third of the way, unburdening us of at least a good half of our load, taking the brooms and the shovels and the buckets upon himself. "My calculations have proven exactly correct, right down to the smallest detail, God be praised." He is delirious. "I am certain it is no more than ten to fifteen meters beneath us. If we begin now and work without ceasing, I'm convinced, with God's help, of course, that we can have it up and running for Rosh Chodesh, the beginning of the new month."

"But friends," he says, handing each of us a shovel and an axe, "this night can't last forever and we have no time to waste!"

And so, we take our stations around Zalman's central marker. I raise my eyes to the great sky, shining high above. I lift the axe they have given me. Physically numb and ravaged by my grief, I begin to dig.

71

We break into the earth with our sharpened hooks, shoveling in deeper with our flat pans. The Hasids sing wordless tunes to keep their spirits up. My back is aching, blisters swell inside my palms. That three old and tired Jews, and one of them dead, can work so

hard is an astonishment to me. Before long, we are knee-deep into the ground, with small hills of overturned dirt all about us. Our shovelfuls are no longer entirely black. They glitter and glisten with silver specks. Pans of dirt fly over our shoulders, bursting apart like shooting stars. Our clothes become covered in silver dust. Indeed, we practically shine.

"Good, good," Zalman mutters happily, confirming everything against his map.

When the ground is to my chest, Zalman strikes something with a hollow clink. The sound chills me to the bone. We relinquish our shovels and congregate, heads together, at the spot.

Zalman whisks away the extraneous dirt with a barber's lathering brush. Digging in with his fingers, he uncovers a long white flute and holds it up to us.

"Bone," he says simply. "Part of an arm, I suspect."

Our work proceeds more slowly after this and with greater care. We must tie handkerchiefs around our faces. With each new shovelful, the pit releases a dram of biting stench. There is no longer any place for us to stand or to walk with safety. We sift through the remains gingerly and in our stocking feet. Despite precautions, our every step breaks something. More than once, one of us puts his foot down and the ground shifts, sending him backwards into the clattering heap.

Had we really convinced ourselves that the moon could be found lying beneath an empty field, ripe for the picking? No, whoever

buried it has buried it deep, beneath layers and layers of corpses, so long ago now that the skin and the muscles have stretched and torn away, and there is nothing left but bones.

Near daybreak, Kalman shouts to us from a distance. Zalman and I make our way through the quicksand of tibias and fibulas, to where the blabbering Kalman is kneeling.

Even after we have reached him, he continues to call our names.

"Kalman, calm down!" Zalman orders.

Kalman points before him, his hand trembling.

Poking out from beneath a cluster of bluish elbows is the tip of the crescent's curved horn, about as big and round as a large man's fedora. It shines with a dull yellow light.

Zalman wraps a tailor's tape around the curving hook and takes its dimensions.

"It must be enormously huge!" I say.

"Judging by the size of the hook," he reads the tape through glasses, "I'd say it's buried fairly deep."

The sun sneaks over the horizon and the moon begins to whiten.

"Quickly," orders Zalman, peering at the sky. "Grab the horn before it disappears!"

Kalman protests. "But, Zalman, I'm exhausted!"

"If it wanes further," says Zalman, "we'll never find it again. Our work will have been for nothing!"

Bleary-eyed, Kalman does as he is told, wrapping his legs and arms around the moon's conical tip.

"Oy, oy, oy, but it's freezing!" he complains.

"You'll get used to it," says Zalman, handing me the end of a long coil of rope. Together, we lash Kalman to his lunar mast.

"But how can I sleep this way?" he calls after us, as we wade to the crater's edge. "I'll be good for nothing this evening! You'll be short a man!"

His words trail us, growing fainter and fainter, as we cross the vast distance, and although I feel sorry for him, I am far too fatigued to be anything but grateful that it is he and not I who must sleep with the sharp hook of the moon rising, like a blade, between his legs.

Zalman and I help each other from the pit. We stand, finally on solid ground, dusting the soil from our trousers. Zalman pours a small bucket of seawater from the spigot in the vat and we wash our hands. My spine aches, my blistered palms are stiff and sore. I have never worked so hard.

Drained, and with one last look at Kalman in the distance, roped now, or so it appears, to a mere column of air, I lie beneath a fir tree. I bend my arm beneath my head and roll onto my side. I hear him shouting and fall instantly asleep.

72

Bing! Ping! Ping! Bing!

I awaken to the pounding of hammers. The sky is black and distant, stained with a milky swirl of stars.

Have I slept the whole day through? It can't be possible!

I sit up, feeling rested and refreshed, if a little sluggish. The moon, low in the field, is half-buried and glowing like a yellow shoe.

So it has neither waned nor freed itself and orbited away.

I rise and move cautiously towards it. Its light is splendid, dazzling. It is immense and I feel like an insignificant dwarf approaching a recumbent queen.

"Look who's risen from the dead, so to speak," Kalman cries out. He is perched atop a complicated scaffolding, near its apex.

Zalman calls down from the opposite side, "Greetings, Reb Chaim." They have braced themselves to these beams with heavy belts. A series of long pipes stretch above the landlocked moon, connecting the scaffolding on either side. The construction must rise nearly sixty feet above the ground. I have to crane my neck to take it in. A thick cable is thrown over the center pipe and a large circular weight dangles from it like a watch on a chain, as though a mesmerist were preparing to hypnotize a giant.

Beneath it, embedded at my feet, the moon glows like a golden beetle stranded on its back, an embroidery of dark veins woven across its belly.

Zalman and Kalman cease their hammering and shimmy down their poles, smiling the serene smiles of accomplishment.

"We tried to awaken you," Zalman says, "but the task proved beyond our meager capabilities."

I sit upon an overturned bucket at the crater's edge. My right leg trembles from disuse. There's nothing I can do to make it stop. I was worn out, it's true.

"You built all this in a single day?" I say, when they are near enough to hear me. It's impossible!

"With God's help," they say.

"And the piping?" Unsteadily, I approach the base of the structure for a closer look. "Where did it come from?" With a curled fist, I knock upon a section of the bluish pipe, sounding out a hollow ring.

Have they built this monstrous contraption out of bones?

Kalman catches up with me.

"As soon as evening came, Zalman released me from guarding the moon. I, too, had slept the entire day. Like yourself. Only I can't tell you the sorts of dreams I had. Try resting sometime with the moon for a pillow. In these dreams, Reb Chaim, I was nothing like myself. There were circular hoops, like bracelets, with beads on them, one black and one white. And they winked at me! And then each hoop jumped into a pair of shoes!"

"But what holds them together?" I say, pushing with my hand against the structure.

Kalman leans in towards me and grins. He removes a work glove with his teeth. "That, only Zalman knows." He raises his head and scratches his beard, looking up at their construction. "But I suspect it's a higher physics of some kind."

73

According to Kalman, Zalman worked tirelessly through the day, carrying heavy tools and machinery, sleeping less than ten minutes every six hours. Although his hair is quite grey, he appears younger than when I first met him, and muscular beneath loose-fitting clothes. Even with the thick belt of tools hanging from his trim middle, he shimmies easily up and down the scaffolding, pulling himself along its narrow beams with a giant fish hook in the crook of his arm.

We stand beneath him on a pier of wooden planks, which the two Hasids constructed while I slept. I can't believe I have missed so much! The pier extends over the pit, so that we may now reach the moon without stepping on anybody's bones. Only the upper surfaces of the planet and it's two horns have been disinterred, the bulk remains hidden as deeply as before. Its buried light shines through the bony sticks surrounding it, illuminating them, seemingly, from within.

From Zalman's height, the whole thing must look like a melon rind tossed upon a garbage heap.

Kalman hands me a section of chain, and, at Zalman's signal, we

carry the stiff coils, unwinding them from a giant spindle, beneath the arches of the scaffolding and to the end of the wooden pier.

"Careful, Reb Chaim," he says. "It can be a little slippery at first."

He plants one foot on the moon's glassy belly and offers me his hand.

Perhaps he sees my hesitation.

"Someone must stay on the pier," he says, "while the other binds the moon in chains. I have not only already walked upon it, but have slept roped to its horn as well."

"All right, all right," I say glumly, wondering why I ever agreed to help in this lunatic adventure? Of what concern is their moon to me? Even were we to return it to the skies, still my nights would be as black as a printer's apron! Nothing will take from me my grief. And yet, I have to admit, the prospect of walking across its lustrous surfaces is alluring. As a boy, I used to dream of it. *An excellent hiding place,* I childishly thought, *if only I could reach it.*

And so I put my hand into Kalman's rough glove and bind a coil of chain around my shoulder. We count together and he yanks me forward, gripping my arm as I pass. Bracing my back, he pushes me along, my feet slipping and sliding, my arms flailing in great wheels.

"Well?" he cries, dropping his hands to his knees.

I am unprepared for how giddy the experience makes me. I can't help laughing. The moon's buttery slopes are icy, slick. "It's like walking on a frozen pond!" I call to him over my shoulder.

My legs shake and tremble, my shoes can find nothing solid to cling to.

Zalman calls encouragements from his high perch on the narrow beam, but to raise my head to search for him, I'm sure, would throw my balance off entirely and send me sliding over the edge into a tumult of exploding shards. So with both arms out on either side for balance, little by little, I adjust my movements, until I'm walking with mincing steps and a straightened spine. The secret, I'm delighted to learn, is skating. Soon I am zooming beneath the scaffolding and across the lunar terrain. How extraordinarily light I've become! My body isn't as bulky here as it is on the earth. Even the heavy chain, once it enters the moon's atmosphere, loses much of its weight. For the sheer sweet joy of it, I drop its heavy coils and gambol and caper like a frisky skater, leaping and spinning around the craters in clumsy figure eights.

"You see, you see!" Kalman calls from the pier. "Now imagine dreaming through that feeling!"

Zalman says, "Because I have absolutely no idea how long you can stay on the moon before freezing into ice yourself, I suggest you stop cavorting, Reb Chaim, and immediately get to work!"

Chastened, I skid back to where I left the chain. Already, it has begun to stick and freeze to the crescent's icy skin.

Kalman skates over with a pair of gloves so that I may pull at the metal without causing pain to my hands. He brings as well my long

woolen scarf, which I drape about my neck. He is panting from the exertion and his breath clouds up in steamy puffs.

Zalman lowers a bucket on the end of the dangling cable. Heads raised, Kalman and I watch it inch its way down like a mischievous spider. Inside we find an assortment of little clips and bars and a harness as well.

"With these," says Zalman, "you will be able to support yourself against the underside."

"You must secure the chain," Kalman adds, "wrapping it across the two horns, so that we may hoist it up."

I look from one to the other. Surely they are jesting.

"This, you want *me* to do?" What do they take me for, a muscle man? "I'm old," I say, "and even as a youngster, I never went in for gymnastics of any kind."

Zalman sits upon the narrow beam as though upon a mighty horse, his legs dangling on either side. "Reb Chaim," he barks, "everyone must do his part!"

He is not standing on the lunar surface with its loony disequilibrium, and so the situation does not strike him as hilariously improbable as it does me. "Because you are dead," he says, "you will be able to last longer in the dark underparts. Kalman and I would freeze there in an instant."

Kalman nods sympathetically. "Have you never climbed a mountain perhaps?"

"Never," I say.

"It's not unlike mountain climbing."

"Which I have never done," I reiterate, shouting disagreeably so that Zalman may hear.

74

From Zalman's dangling bucket, Kalman removes the harness, which he straps through my legs and around my waist. With a metal clip, he buckles me to the long chain.

"This will free your hands, for the climbing."

He tucks two additional clips, one into each of my coat pockets, and gives them both a little pat.

I feel as though I'm being diapered by a disapproving nanny.

The bucket offers other treasures: a pair of pointed hammers, two railroad spikes, boots with rows of spiked teeth across the toes and heels.

According to Kalman, I am to curl like a worm along the upper and lower surfaces of the moon's great horns, digging in with my feet, hoisting myself along with my arms, and pulling the chain behind me like a thread.

"The difficult part," Kalman says, "will be pushing through the bones."

He leads me to the edge.

"We suggest you proceed feet first," calls Zalman.

"With your belly flat against the moon."

Zalman assures me, "This is the most efficient procedure." He is growing impatient with my delays, I can tell.

Kalman returns to the pier and to the large spindle on which the lengths of chain are coiled.

"I'll be here at the spindle, letting out the chain. Should anything untoward happen—"

"Which it will not!" interjects Zalman, from above.

"Which it will not," repeats Kalman, "but if, God forbid, it does, I have only to reel you in and you'll be perfectly safe again on the pier."

There is no gentlemanly way out, and so I kneel on the far side and look over the moon's glossy edge. It is cold against my knees, and the sensation makes me laugh. However, under Zalman's scrutiny, I suppress my hilarity. I turn, so that I'm facing Kalman, and lower my abdomen against the moon's slick hide. It burns with a sharp sting and I very nearly lose consciousness.

"Easy," Zalman cautions. "Take it slowly. Allow your body to adjust."

Kalman makes the chain taut, until it pulls over my head and against my back. I take the railroad spikes, one in each hand, and force them into the crunchy soil. My body is now pressing entirely against the moon. What little blood I have rushes to my head. A tickling from someplace beneath the surface caresses my belly in waves. I can feel it through my coat and my vest. It's as

though a thousand tiny fish were puckering my skin, their tingling kisses bringing with them a pervasive warmth. I cry out involuntarily.

"What?" shouts a concerned Zalman.

"It's nothing, nothing!" I shout back.

I descend an arm's length, crunching knee-deep into the sea of bones.

75

Narrowing my eyes, I lower my head in, chin first, my mouth tightly shut, my own skull disappearing beneath the others. The skeletal mass is not as dense as I had feared, and I am able to sink into it, scrambling down and clinging to the moon's glistening side with my spikes.

"It's only me," I whisper. "You needn't be afraid."

Her gentle light, through the weave of dry bones, is not without its beauty. Skulls stare at me with darkened sockets, grimacing through gnashed or broken teeth. With each of my blind steps, bones rattle and crunch, shifting to make room, their sounds reaching my ears as though through water.

"You cannot stay here," I tell her. "You mustn't punish yourself. What good does it do, hiding in such a desolate place?"

Down, down, down I go, and it isn't long before I'm dangling

beneath her jagged spine. I release the spikes from one side, attaching them to the other. My arms and my elbows ache. "Don't drop me," I plead. Hanging by one arm to her chine, I reach into my pockets for the pointed hammers. Arching my back, I struggle, biting in with my spiked boots, throwing hammers wildly above my head.

The first revolution around the thickest part of her girth is, of course, the longest. Girdling her in chains, I am up and out finally, crawling along on my hands and knees, collapsing upon her bosom.

Kalman and Zalman cheer. Kalman steps near to assist me.

"Should he take a break?"

"Do you need a break, Reb Chaim?"

"How does he feel?"

"How do you feel?"

"Fine, fine," I cry, rotating my arms and sitting up, while Kalman dusts bone fragments from my clothing.

With Kalman's aid, I tighten the first loop of chain around the hooked tip and fasten it with clips. Kneeling again, I climb around again, and then again, three revolutions, with Kalman easing the chain carefully from his spindle. I repeat the process on the other side, inching myself along the underbelly with my spikes and my hammer tongs, until the moon is laced in six strong loops of chain.

"And now how do you feel, Reb Chaim?" Zalman shouts down.

"Very cold," I say. "But, curiously, also warm. There's a quality of warmth underneath, from inside."

"From the source of its light, I imagine," he says.

Kalman unlocks the chain from my waist, he removes the harness, and I'm invited to sit on the pier with my feet in a bucket of steaming water, wrapped in five heavy blankets. Kalman slides agilely to the center of the moon's curving surface. There, he stands on a stepladder and raises the chain high above his head, linking it to Zalman's suspended hook.

76

Zalman descends from the narrow bar. Kalman skates back to his place on the pier, carrying the stepladder with him. Hastily, I dry my feet and return them to my shoes. I don't want to miss anything. Except for a soreness in my upper back and forearms, I'm feeling quite myself again.

The two brothers-in-law practically run to the edge of the forest where, with a pair of needle-nose pliers, Kalman makes the final adjustments on a grimy motorized winch. Where all this machinery comes from, I have no idea. I cross my arms and wait for further instructions. Zalman murmurs a blessing and then, bracing his foot against the machine, pulls the ripcord with all his

might. The motor starts up with a barking cough, before shuddering back into cold silence. Zalman yanks the cord once more, but the machine only splutters reluctantly. On the third pull, some essential thing ignites within it and the motor roars like an impatient bull.

Grunting with satisfaction, Zalman wipes the grease from his hands on a dirty chamois. He opens the throttle, adjusts a latch. The spiral bevels bite into each other, reeling the steel cable in, until the chain loses all its slack. The motor grinds against the resistance of the moon's great weight.

"Easy, careful now," Zalman whispers to himself, monitoring the winch's speed.

Slowly, the bones give way and the moon is lifted up. The winch grinds without hurry until the crescent is finally exposed, suspended in its chains. Bones drop from it like water from a hooked whale. My eyes accustom themselves to its intense new light. The bright opalescence engraves deep shadows into the faces of my two companions. Soon, however, it becomes apparent that the moon's surfaces are not clear, but have been mottled, as though with dark and purple bruises.

"The core is spongy, as opposed to its harder, icier crusts," Zalman says when I draw his attention to these discolorations. "It must've drawn the blood into itself."

The sight nauseates me.

"Luckily, we brought push brooms," says Kalman, presenting one to each of us. He and Zalman exchange sly smiles: to their minds, nothing has been left to chance. God has provided for everything.

We return to the pier with the brooms.

In the vat where I steamed my feet, Kalman now prepares a brew of seawater and silt. The moon hangs, quavering, a few feet above our heads, beetling like a hoisted boat. Following Kalman's lead, I dip the bristles of my brush into the briny vat and raise the broom against the moon's curved side. Zalman does this as well, each of us concentrating on a different section. Standing on the stepladders when we need them, we scrub and we rub, and although the mottling lightens, the stain is too deep. Our burnishing cannot make it disappear. Again on ladders and with dark glasses to protect our eyes, we rub the moon down, drying it with towels until it gleams even more brightly than before, despite the mottling. Forever now, the moon will appear this way, no longer the smooth and gleaming pearl I remember from my youth.

Also, I can't help commenting on the many pockmarks its surface has sustained.

"Bullet holes," is Zalman's grim-lipped reply.

We climb off our ladders and fold them away. The brooms we store upon our cart, leaning them against the vat of seawater. I rub

my hands together. They are coarse and dry with blisters. All that remains now is to return the moon to its niche in the proper quadrant of the sky. Kalman must be thinking the same thing, for together, we turn to Zalman, who stands upon the pier, his arms hugging one another, as though he were shivering.

He meets our gazes. "Gentlemen," he says, pinching at his sleeves, "I have no idea how to proceed."

77

"Perhaps," Kalman suggests, "if we untie the chains, the moon may float on its own into place."

Dark planes shift across Zalman's hawk-like face. He shrugs gloomily. "Nothing I understand of the process gives me any confidence an approach of that sort will succeed."

I clear my throat. "May I suggest we recite the sanctification over the moon. Whether it helps or not, surely it wouldn't be inappropriate."

Zalman's spirits seem to lift, if only slightly, and the three of us gather close together. At first, however, no one can remember the words of the prayer, so long has it been since anyone had cause to recite them.

"How does it begin?" I ask. "Does anyone remember?"

78

"Hallelujah, praise God?" This is Kalman's shy suggestion.

"That's it!" Zalman cries and immediately the sentences flow into the dried riverbeds of our brains.

"Hallelujah! Praise God," our voices rise as one. "Praise God from the sky, praise Him in the Heavens! Praise Him all His angels, praise Him all His Hosts! Praise Him sun and moon, praise Him stars of light. Praise Him skies of skies, and the waters above the skies!"

The words burst from our dammed hearts. And at the appropriate passage, we address the moon itself, quivering above us, so near.

"Blessed be your Former, your Maker, your Possessor, your Creator!" We repeat the formula the required three times.

"Just as I leap towards you but cannot touch you," we say, leaping into the air, "may my enemies not touch me with their evil! Let them fall from dread and terror! Let them be as still as stones!"

We turn to one another and exchange the traditional greeting, "Peace to you. And to you, great peace," our eyes moist with tears.

"Let every soul praise God," we whisper. "Let every soul praise God."

We utter the rest of the psalms and benedictions, our arms bracing one another for support.

"The Eternal will bless us, all peoples of the earth, all peoples of the earth. Amen."

At Zalman's directive, we station ourselves at key positions, near

the clips that fasten the chains in which the moon is bound. Zalman himself climbs aboard the moon's gleaming prow, planting his feet in the middle. On the count of three, Kalman and I release the clips from the twin horns. The chains unravel and fall from the moon like clattering snakes. The moon rocks perilously and we scramble for firm ground. Zalman, balancing himself, barely has time to release the hook and jump to the pier, before the crescent crashes with the smashing force of gravity, sending bone fragments flying in all directions.

"Look out!"

We turn against the bony gale, teeth and knuckles pelting our backs, pounding into us like hail stones.

When it's safe to look, the moon is once again stranded in its bed, a pregnant woman who cannot lift herself without assistance.

"Zalman, Zalman, I'm so sorry!" I say, running to him.

But my words are ridiculous and small. Absurd to comfort Zalman, as though this enterprise were his alone.

He sits on an overturned bucket, his back bent, his beard in his hands, staring at the luminous wreck before him.

I doubt he even hears me.

79

I myself am about to sit, when, nearby, a tree limb breaks. Its cracking and peeling, familiar to me from a life in the lumber business,
fills the air and a metallic voice cries out "God in Heaven be
praised!!! Whooooooo!!!"

I search the tree line. Against the starry patterns of night, the
black outline of a figure can be seen spiraling to the ground.

By the time we reach him, at the far end of the field, the man is
up, limping in small circles, attempting to dust the debris of the
forest from his black and somber clothing. My hopes of seeing my
Rebbe are once again dashed. This man is far too old and with a
whitened head, too delicate and so very frail.

"Old man, what were you doing in the trees?" I ask, offering an
arm for him to lean on, while Kalman and Zalman brush the leaves
and pine cones from his shoulders.

"Chaimka," he says. "It's me!"

The voice has grown reedy with age, but it is unmistakably his.
He raises his burning blue eyes, so bright I can see them even in this
dark, and looks at me from beneath the brim of his black fedora.
The skin, tightening against sharp cheekbones, creates a rueful
smile.

"Once again, don't you even know your own Rebbe?"

"Rebbe?" I say. But it cannot be! Surely, this is not my Rebbe,

but his own father, or even his grandfather, both of whom were saints. "Rebbe, how old you have become!" I say. No, it's impossible. It's as though an artist had sketched over his portrait with chalk, whitening the outline and all the small details. His frame remains thin and vigorously upright, it's true, but he must be nearing ninety!

"Stop gawking, Chaimka," he says. "It's me. It's me."

The two Hasids and I escort our revered master to the bucket, where we make him sit, despite his protest that nothing is the matter. Kalman prepares a glass of water, which the Rebbe drinks awkwardly, spilling a line across his snowy beard. With the back of his hand, he pats the spot until it's dry.

"I'll get used to it again," he chirps. "I'll get used to it again."

He stands and stretches his arms, folding them behind his back.

"Now what do we have here, what do we have here?" He warbles this, strutting to the edge of the pit, his beak-like nose leading him there. He turns his head sharply, this way and that, from one horn of the moon to the other.

"Who can explain this?"

He looks over his shoulder through one cold eye.

"Rebbe," Zalman steps forward. "We followed the map, which I devised."

"Followed the map? Good, good," the Rebbe clacks.

"After waiting for Reb Chaim."

"Exactly as you specified," Kalman forces his way into the conversation, hungry for the Rebbe's attention and his praise.

"He appeared, as I said he would, did he not?" the Rebbe nods.

"Exactly according to your exact specifications," Kalman repeats needlessly.

"We excavated the pit," Zalman says without pride.

"Yes, I see, very good."

"The moon was there, beneath the bones."

"Beneath the bones, yes, I see," the Rebbe's eyes sparkle, catching the light of the moon. Although Zalman may berate himself, that he managed to achieve even this much is not insignificant, and the Rebbe is obviously pleased.

"I slept on it, Rebbe," Kalman offers, a clumsy attempt to garner more attention for himself, "so that it not disappear."

"You slept on it, did you, Reb Kalman?"

"Yes, Rebbe, I did."

"In chains, I suppose?"

"Yes, Rebbe."

"Ah, what dreams you must have had, what dreams!" the Rebbe looks at him directly.

"Hoops, Rebbe, I dreamt of hoops."

"Ah, yes, the hoops, the hoops! Remind me to tell you of my own experiences one day."

"Yes, Rebbe," says Kalman, stepping back. "I will very much enjoy hearing of them."

"But now, as you can see, Rebbe," Zalman interrupts, doggedly putting forth his despairing account. "The moon is free, but we have been unable to force it to rise."

"You recited the benedictions?"

"Of course."

"At Reb Chaim's suggestion," Kalman adds, in a showy display of generosity.

"Hmm . . . Well, then, this is a complicated matter."

The Rebbe circumnavigates the pit with vigorous strides. We have difficulty keeping up with him and tag along in an uncertain gaggle, waiting to supply whatever information he might need.

Every now and again, he stops and fixes his eyes upon the sunken crescent. During these intervals, we also cease our walking, the three of us, and gaze ignorantly at the moon, hoping to see there whatever the Rebbe himself is seeing.

"Chaimka," his thin voice finally calls to me and, for a moment, I hear in it the familiar raven's clack.

"Yes, Rebbe?" I leave the two Hasids and join him. The moon lies, swollen, at our feet. I am a head taller than my Rebbe and, for the life of me, as I watch his face now, standing behind him, I find it impossible to believe he ever was a crow.

"Chaimka," this the Rebbe says, so quietly and almost like a child. "Hold my coat so I don't fall in."

The Rebbe's shoe dislodges a small stone that jumps over the edge and into the pile of broken bones. The little rock dances, ping-

ing against one hollow stick to the next, before spinning down a crack and disappearing for good.

"I understand," I say.

With the Rebbe leaning over the edge of the pit, I dig in my heels, keeping the tails of his long black coat bunched together in both hands, so that neither he nor I fall in.

Raising his arms, the Rebbe shouts, "In the name of God, and with the merit of my righteous ancestors, I command you, O fallen luminary, to return to your place in the Heavens above!"

Zalman and Kalman move near. They stand behind us, peeking over each other's shoulders. The Rebbe takes three steps back and smoothes down the wrinkled tails of his jacket.

The moon grinds and chafes against the bones, as though waking from a slumber. Slowly, it begins to float and soon is swaying above our heads, bathing us in its light. If the wind happened to blow it even slightly in our direction, we might be crushed, should it fall. And for a moment, my heart grows faint with terror. But no, it ascends steadily, lurching from side to side, gaining momentum and speed.

I recall Ola's telescope, and hurry to my bag, running with the moon behind my back. Ahead of me, my shadow dances across the ground, shortening as the moon draws itself further and further away. I open my bag and extract the spyglass and return with it as quickly as I can. We pass the collapsible cylinder among ourselves, watching the moonrise through its fractured lens. It sails as if by instinct to its proper quadrant. This, Zalman verifies against his map with our compass.

Finally, it comes to a rest. I have no idea how much time has passed, but not a little.

Still, none of us moves to leave. We bend our necks back and keep our heads lifted to the sky.

I cannot say I experience much joy and, judging from their stern and melancholy countenances, neither do my companions. Curious, after all this work.

"But how can we be sure," Kalman whispers fretfully, "that it won't wax and wane and disappear again?"

No one, not even the Rebbe, answers him and his words bring with them a mood of finality. They signal an end, not only to our work, but to our observations as well. We stretch, cracking our stiff joints and bending our backs until they pop. This one kneels to tie a shoe, that one blows his nose. With the tip of my handkerchief, I wipe spittle from the corner of my mouth. Zalman and Kalman collect the spare ends of their machinery and their equipment, and begin packing it away. Periodically, each of us glances nervously at the moon, reassured and haunted by its presence in the sky.

"Chaimka," the Rebbe calls, turning away. "Stay near now. Our work is not yet over for the night."

80

There is nothing, really, left for us to say, and so I bid farewell to my two companions. I can see their weariness, in Zalman's red-rimmed eyes, in Kalman's sagging shoulders. They're exhausted and why shouldn't they be? This in itself might account for the simplicity of our farewells. But something else, a throbbing heaviness, enters into our exchanges, as we grasp each other by the hand and offer our tired kisses. They are at the end of fifty years of work, fifty-odd years of waiting, of planning, of study and interpretation. Hardly a simple task to awaken in the morning and prepare tea, contemplating the day's few meaningless chores.

And what have we really accomplished? The moon once again shines, it's true, but its resistance to our gravity is perhaps rather tenuous. I mustn't speak for my companions, but it's hard to feel that anything has changed. Also, we are each perhaps humiliated and a little ashamed to have spent so much time in such extraordinary darkness. And so our farewells, as I say, are passed between us hastily, like cards in a game of Sixty-Six.

The Rebbe approaches as we finish our goodbyes. He takes my arm and escorts me away, but turns back without me for a few private words.

As I watch the three of them talk, a longing pierces my heart. How will I face tomorrow without them, my two dear Hasids?

"Of course, of course," I hear Zalman saying.

The Rebbe returns, leaving them to their packing. They must dismantle their structures. On the Rebbe's instructions, they will return after a short rest to replace the bones and cover them again with earth.

The night is thick. There is no hint of morning in the air. The Rebbe and I walk away from the moon, our blue shadows slanting at our feet. Behind us, the clanging and banging sounds of the two Hasids disassembling their equipment start to fade. I think I hear them shouting at us, as they pull their cart away, but I cannot really be certain.

"We don't always understand God's ways," the Rebbe is saying. "But that is our failing, not His."

His voice is clear, like the sound of moving waters.

"I have tried my best to assist you but, of course, there were things you had to do on your own. You have done these things now, Chaim. You have done the necessary things. Don't try to understand them."

A blue light floods through the trees and a lumbering weariness overtakes me. I can barely lift one foot after the other. My shoes feel weighted with lead. When I fear I will not be able to walk another step, the Rebbe indicates, through a small gesture of his head, that we may stop. My chest is constricted and I must lean against a tree for support.

"Ah, Chaimka," he says, approaching me, digging with his fingers into a pocket of his vest. He is a trim man still, his chest a narrow

column above an indented belly. As I watch his hand, I am flooded with revulsion for him.

"Don't come near me!" I scream, shocked by my own words.

"Chaimka, you have worked so hard," he murmurs. "So hard. I'm going to help you now."

The Rebbe lifts a bony, yellowed hand and places it against my chest. My dormant heart begins pounding in wild spasms. I want to run away, but can't.

"Rebbe," is the only word I can manage. Sweat pours from me, my forehead and my shirt are drenched in it, my chest. My tongue sits, thick and dry, in the cavity of my mouth, like a shoehorn someone has forced into it.

"Try not to struggle, sheyne, sha, sha," the Rebbe mews. "Rest, rest. You have earned it. Let me help you. I am your Rebbe, after all. The pangs of the grave have ended."

The Rebbe has fallen beneath me, his thin knees brace the side of my body, his chest presses against my back. He places one warm hand on my heart, a wild fluttering bird, and the other on my forehead. His thumb finds the space of skin between my eyes. I understand that I will die.

"No, no, not die, not die, hush, hush," he whispers, reading my every thought. "That happened long ago, long ago." His familiar voice is again soothing. With difficulty, I twist my neck to find his face, for its comfort, but also to assure him that the disgust I felt was of the moment only and not authentic, but I can barely

move my body. Such a strain it is to lift my head. And when I am able finally to roll over, he isn't there. In his place is a young woman, a girl really. I am lying on her square and enormous lap. Her black hair is wild and untied, it falls into her face, a face I know, but which I have never seen so young.

"Chaimka, Chaimka," she sings. "Do you know me? Can you say my name?"

My history falls away, like sacks of grain from a careless farmer's wagon. I begin to forget everything. Names of trees . . . times of day . . . the words of the morning prayer . . . the Bund . . . details of leases, of mortgages . . . the purpose and function of cravats, of wine, of air . . . all remove themselves, one by one, from my understanding. Beneath this large woman's caressing hands, I forget my children's names. Even their faces leave me. I no longer recall how I earned my living or why I died. I'm floating, free from detail, although I find I can still, without difficulty, remember my name.

Chaim Skibelski.

"Chaimka, Chaimka," the woman sings, "look at the moon. Can you see the moon?"

My small body is flooded with well-being. I gurgle in her lap. With her large fingers, she carefully turns my head and the light of the moon fills my eyes, until it is all I see.

A BLESSING ON THE MOON

BY JOSEPH SKIBELL

B

An Interview with Joseph Skibell

QUESTION: *Is it true that your novel started out as a play?*

SKIBELL: Well, not as a play exactly, but as a monologue in a play that I was writing at the time and which, incidentally, I have never finished. The play was about a character very much like myself, coming to terms with the effect his aunts' and uncles' and great-grandparents' deaths in the Holocaust have had on him. At one point, the ghost of the main character's great-grandfather enters the stage, gunshot wounds in his face, et cetera, et cetera, very dramatic, you know, and he starts to speak. I had written this scene maybe fifteen times and was totally stuck. The whole play simply could not get over the hump of this one scene. (It still hasn't). Anyway, the great-grandfather's character recalls the day he died, the day the Germans roared into town, rounding up Jews and shooting them in the forest. And to my horror — or to my additional horror, apart from the subject matter — I saw that the character wasn't even speaking in dialogue. It was prose! I did everything I could to turn my great-grandfather's words into stage dialogue.

QUESTION: *Like what?*

SKIBELL: I added "ums" and "uhs," I had him repeating words, stuttering, things like that. But there was no denying it: the monologue was in prose.

QUESTION: *So what did you do with it?*

SKIBELL: I didn't know what to do with it. I kept it, fortunately. I filed it away in an ever fattening file of rejected drafts of an impossible scene in an unwritable play, and then, one day, it occurred to me that I could perhaps turn it into a short story. I had seen a notice for a

short story contest and was trying my hand at the form, and I thought this might make a good little story. So I took the monologue out of the file, dusted out all the "ums" and "uhs," the speechy repetitions and whatnot, and when I sat down to write, the whole story came pouring through me. In one very intense sitting. In fact,

I can remember getting to one particularly appalling detail, the gifts exchanged by the Polish family around the breakfast table the morning after they move into my great-grandparents' house — and I myself was appalled and sickened as the words appeared on the page, as though I were not the scene's writer but its first reader. It was only about one thousand words, but by the time I got to the end, I was exhausted.

QUESTION: *But how did it become a novel?*

SKIBELL: Well, as soon as I wrote the closing period, the first sentence of what became the second chapter ("The Rebbe is not his usual self") presented itself to my inner ear, but there was no way I could continue writing. So I kept that sentence buzzing around in my aural safe-deposit box for a few months, and it eventually launched the second chapter, and ultimately the book.

QUESTION: *In the book, the fantastic elements are so...*

SKIBELL: Weird?

QUESTION: *Yeah: dead Jews, talking animals. Did that weirdness just leap out at you during that intense hour of writing?*

SKIBELL: Well, for years I've been a great lover of fairy tales and folk tales. Yiddish folk tales, especially, speak to me. It's my culture, after all. And I guess I had been soaking my consciousness in them for so long that a story with talking animals and Rabbis turning into birds and Jews unable to get into the World to Come didn't seem that strange to me. Also, it always struck me how much the Holocaust (which, to some extent, is the invisible backdrop to my childhood) seemed foreshadowed in the tales of the Brothers Grimm: the oven in Hansel and Gretal becomes the ovens of Auschwitz; the Pied Piper

leading away the rats and then the children of Hamelin is, to me, the story of World War II. Hitler as the mesmerizing entrancer seducing the "rats" — which is how the Nazis characterized European Jewry — to their doom; the bad faith of the German people; the loss of their children, the next generation, who suffer the consequence of their bad faith: what is that if not the story of the Holocaust? And, believe me, after 150 years of "The Jew in the Thornbush" as a bedtime tale, nothing the Germans did should come as a surprise. So, anyway, I always had this idea, I had always made that connection, but I didn't really want to work through the medium of German folk tales. And when I eventually discovered the great wealth of Jewish and Yiddish tales, I knew I had found my form.

QUESTION: *A moment ago, you called the Holocaust the "invisible backdrop to my childhood." Can you explain?*

SKIBELL: Yeah, I guess...I don't know. Although my parents were American, I grew up surrounded by great-aunts and -uncles and my grandparents, who were all European. My grandfather and his brothers were the sons of Chaim Skibelski. Chaim had had ten children. All of his daughters and one of his sons died in the war, and also all their children. My grandfather escaped, as did my uncle Sidney, who fled Poland with his wife, Regina, and wound up in a Soviet work camp, which was nearly as bad as a German concentration camp. Eventually, they made it to America, after the war. All in all, about eighteen members of our immediate family had just disappeared, violently, from the face of the earth. And no one ever talked about it. This silence, I think, haunted me as a child and formed my character in a number of ways which eventually were not that pleasing to me. So the book is an attempt on my part to recover from the silence a family history that, except for a clutch of photos and whatever is encoded genetically, has all but disappeared. It's an imaginative reconstruction, of course, not a historical one, and because of that, I feel it is somehow truer. In any case, through this imaginative reconstruction, I've gotten to spend two very intimate years, primarily with my great-grandfather, but also with my great-grandmother, and my great-uncles and -aunts and cousins, through writing this book. They've taught me a lot.

QUESTION: *Would you characterize the novel as a book of forgiveness?*

SKIBELL: That's a complex issue. As Chaim says to the head of the German soldier, "You've taken everything from me. Must you have my forgiveness as well?" It's not really up to me to forgive. Or not completely, anyway. I can only forgive the effect it's had on me. Most of the ones who could forgive have been dead for fifty years and soon most of the ones who need forgiveness will be dead as well. Have the culpable ones even asked for forgiveness? Not only for what was done to the Jews, but to the whole world. I feel the world suffered a tremendous blow. I don't know, I don't know. In Jewish thought, we are taught to look at everything that happens to us as a blessing. Good or bad. There is only one God, after all, who is the source of everything, so everything is a blessing. Or should be seen as such. It's not always easy to do that, I know. In any case, I hope this book is a book of blessing.

* Reprinted with permission from the June '97 issue of The Algonkian

*The following questions, discussion topics, and notes are intended to enhance your reading of **A Blessing on the Moon** and to provide additional material to facilitate your group's discussion.*

1. How does the author establish the fantastical nature of the novel from its very beginning? Why do you think the author utilized the plot device of turning the Rebbe into a crow? Why does this metamorphosis seem appropriate for the character? How does the first sentence of chapter two, "The Rebbe is not his usual self, that much is clear" (p.8), establish the mood and set up the action for part one of the book?

2. Chaim laments, "Without the moon, who can keep track of the time?" (p. 204). How does the author play with time as the novel progresses? How does this technique affect the way we experience Chaim's story? What is the significance of the 50 years that elapse during the course of the book?

3. Chaim is a man of almost unflinching faith, who believes, "What's forbidden is forbidden" (p. 236) and says, "If the Rebbe insists, who am I to argue?" (p. 228). How does Chaim's adherence to Jewish law both simplify and complicate his existence? What are his feelings about the stringent Hasidic beliefs he witnesses by observing Kalman and Zalman? How does their discussion of whether the Law permits them to take the abandoned boat (pp. 111-114) foreshadow the events of the novel's conclusion?

4. Most of the characters are able to see the dead Chaim, but to others he and his blood are invisible. Who can see him, and who cannot? Why do you think the author decided to make him invisible to some? What is significant about the parts of the story during which Chaim bleeds? How and when are towels used as a ritual for cleansing and healing (see pp. 71, 135, and 254)?

5. What is the nature of the attraction between Chaim and Ola? Why does Chaim succumb to "what is forbidden" in this relationship? Why is he reluctant to reveal to her the truth about death (pp. 43-44)? What are Ola's greatest gifts to Chaim?

6. The themes of abandonment and loss are ubiquitous in the novel, and Chaim often exclaims, "What can God be thinking!" If God could answer Chaim, how do you think their conversation would progress? How would Ola, the Rebbe, Ester, Ida, and others explain to Chaim their own "abandonment" of him?

7. The Hotel Amfortas is a unique and colorful representation of Chaim's idea of paradise. Describe your own version of the ideal "Hotel Amfortas" and the events that would take place there. How do the similarities and differences illuminate the similarities and differences between you and the character of Chaim Skibelski?

8. What are the first clues that something is amiss at the Hotel Amfortas? How does the hotel's deterioration mirror the events and outcome of the Holocaust? What happens to Chaim physically and psychologically as the hotel falls into ruin (pp. 190-196)?

9. Explore the symbolism of the moon's burial beneath layers of corpses and the construction of the scaffolding from human bones held together by "a higher physics of some kind" (p. 244). Who was responsible for pulling the moon down from the sky in the first place? Is there more than one answer to this question?

10. The release of the moon from its burial site is simultaneous with the release of Chaim at the novel's climax. What does this transition require of Chaim, and how does he react at first? Do you think Ola would have been comforted if she had known what happens to Chaim on the last page of the book? Do you think Ola underwent a similar process? Why, or why not?

11. Chaim notes the blood and pockmarks that mar the moon's surface as it is about to be restored to its rightful place: "Forever now, the moon will appear this way, no longer the smooth and gleaming pearl I remember from my youth" (p. 254). How have the events of the Holocaust changed forever the way the world appears, and how might the preceding quotation begin to suggest the feelings of the descendants of those who died at the hands of Hitler's army? What does Chaim mean when he says, "Many worlds have been lost, not simply my own" (p. 219)?

12. While carrying the head of the German soldier, Chaim wonders, "Perhaps I would have been happier being born a wolf" (p. 119). Why does he momentarily feel he would be better off as a vicious animal? What does this fantasy reveal about his feelings toward his killers? About his own character? About his identity as a Jew? Why does he eventually relinquish this fantasy?